Table of Contents

AF423550

To Dezarae, my inspiration for this novel, and who thankfully, never encountered a Dastardly Damned! Thank you for also guiding me through the world of Creepy Pasta and educating me on Slender Man.

Dirty Diana

by Andrea Smith

Copyright © 2022.
Andrea Smith dba Meatball Taster Publishing, LLC
All rights reserved.

All rights reserved. Except as permitted under the U.S. Copyright Act of 1976, no part of this publication may be reproduced, distributed, or transmitted in any form or by any means (electronic, mechanical, photocopying, recording, or otherwise) or stored in a database or retrieval system without the written permission of the author.

The scanning, uploading, and distribution of this book via the Internet or via other means without the permission of the publisher is illegal and punishable by law. Please purchase only licensed authorized electronic editions, and please do not encourage electronic piracy sites where authors' books are illegally offered for free. This is known as pirating. This is illegal.

Thank you for respecting the hard work of this author.

This book is a work of fiction. Any resemblance to actual persons, living or dead, events, or locations is purely coincidental.

Prologue

FALL OF 2014

Diana Webster was the last one off the school bus, just like always. Her older brother, Alex, was walking with his right arm around Liz, his girlfriend, paying no attention to his younger sister.

And why should he?

He was seventeen, almost eighteen and a super jock in his senior year at Woodrow Wilson High School. Add to that the fact he was going steady with the equally popular femme fatale of WW High, Elizabeth Nolan, made him the real deal of the family.

Alex and Liz were perfect for one another. That was obvious to Diana, just as much as it was obvious to every other student and faculty member at the high school.

Both carried themselves with confidence, because the only thing they had lacking was insecurity. They had looks, status, popularity, acceptance, and intelligence—everything most teens found partially or completely lacking during their formative years.

High school could be brutal.

Especially to a sophomore.

In particular, to Diana Webster, a tenth grade loner who lacked all of the positive attributes her older brother possessed and then some.

What was even worse was that Diana knew that in two more years, by the time she was a senior in high school just like her brother was now, nothing would have changed that significantly. She was almost sixteen. She should've been a junior, but she'd been held back a year when she'd contracted a bad case of mono while in the sixth grade and missed eight weeks of school.

Totally a social outcast as a result.

She knew it.

Her parents knew it.

And if Diana had any friends, they would have been blunt enough to tell her as much. No use in her having any illusions of grandeur. Sometimes the plain truth was best accepted.

Her parents needn't have sprung all those thousands of dollars on braces for her. Perfect teeth weren't going to open any more doors for her socially; nor would they automatically garner the self-confidence her parents knew she was lacking. They tried so hard to promote her self-confidence with their constant compliments on what a beautiful young woman she was morphing into almost daily.

She knew it was bullshit. Everything in her mind assured her of that, and if it didn't, her social status at school confirmed it. Aside from the braces, she had attempted to remove everyone's focus away from her face by dying her hair purple. The problem was, it was a home dye job that had gone horribly wrong, and the purple looked more like a putrid shade of grey.

Diana didn't put forth any effort to change that. Why should she? These were the same students she had gone to school with since moving to Reedsville, Idaho when she was in the second grade. Apparently, they still hadn't come to accept her. It was because she was different and she knew it. She didn't pretend to be anything else.

Being different wasn't something she did intentionally; it wasn't some attention-grabbing mechanism that she had employed to appear as some unique prodigy or enigma. It was simply who she was, and she wasn't about to change for anything or anyone. If that meant she remained a loner? Then so be it.

She enjoyed the company she kept, even though it stressed her parents because she wasn't living up to what they thought was normal teen behavior for their only daughter. They wanted her to be popular—like Alex. To have friends, maybe even a crush or two on boys in her class.

But Diana wasn't into boys - at least not the ones in her sophomore classes. They were so immature with only one thing on their minds—sex.

It wasn't as if Diana was even noticed much by her male classmates. She was quiet; kept to herself most of the time, keeping busy with her sketches and drawings during Study Hall. Diana was artistic, and her passion outside of gaming was creating characters she hoped to someday sell for interactive games she would create. She'd heard there was big money in that, and it would be a perfect way to earn a living by doing the very things she was passionate about.

Gaming was Diana's other guilty pleasure once homework and chores were done each day. She escaped to the solace of her pink-walled room, powered up her laptop, and joined the community of friends she had never met. It didn't matter though, because her online friends never judged her, nor could they tease her relentlessly for being different.

Because they were different too.

She found comfort in her anonymity, and instead of her normal bashful persona, she found that she could easily chat and blend in with the others. Online, they were all equals. There was a mutual respect among them. It was one of the chat room requirements that everyone show respect and manners while gaming or chatting with one another. No harassment or bullying was allowed. And so far, she had not encountered anything but friendly banter and newly made friendships.

She went to her room and sat at her desk, opening her backpack and pulling her books out. The sooner she finished her homework, the sooner she could escape into the gaming world and chat rooms that provided the social interaction she found most rewarding.

Her mother would be home from work by six o'clock, with whatever takeout she felt like picking up for dinner.

It wasn't that Diana was too young to cook, or unwilling to cook, her mother simply didn't trust her in the kitchen. One near disaster with dripping grease onto a burner and then trying to pat out the flames with a cotton dish towel wasn't the smartest thing to do. Her mother didn't want her near the stove unless she was right there next to her to supervise her every move. That part about her mother really sucked.

Diana's father, on the other hand, was totally laid back, or maybe it just seemed that way because he traveled on business and was gone days and sometimes weeks at a time. Maybe that was why her mother felt she needed to pick up the slack for his absence by overly exerting her parental authority. The truth was, Alex was the one who looked out for her the most. And Diana felt closer to Alex than she did her parents.

Diana focused on finishing her homework, and once she was finished, she dutifully placed everything back in her backpack so it would be ready and waiting the following morning. She went into the kitchen where Alex was nuking some popcorn and carrying on a conversation with Liz on his cell. She rolled her eyes as she opened the fridge and grabbed a cold soda. She couldn't, for the life of her, figure out why her brother couldn't go ten minutes without talking to Liz.

"You're going to spoil your dinner, Alex," she warned as if that would matter to him. "Just sayin.'"

"Hey shrimp, I forgot to tell you," he said moving his mouth away from his smart phone, "Mom's picking up Dad at the airport. They're having dinner on the way back, so it'll be after eight when they get home. We lucked out, I'm ordering pizza for us."

She shrugged heading back out of the kitchen, "Pepperoni and mushrooms," she hollered over her shoulder.

"Yeah, yeah, you think I don't know that by now?" her brother called after her.

So, their father was coming home tonight. She hadn't even been aware of that. It was the norm to be kept in the dark about his schedule. Diana couldn't count the number of birthdays and Christmases he had missed over the years. And she didn't know a whole lot about his job because they weren't supposed to know about it. He worked for the government. All she knew for sure was that he traveled to other states, and sometimes to other countries, for unspecified amounts of time to ensure national security.

Period.

But Diana was okay with not knowing more than that because if she did, she was pretty sure she would spend most of her time worrying about him.

Just like her mom did.

Oh, her mother tried to not let it show, but Diana didn't miss the occasions when days or weeks went by with no word from her father. Her mother would mope at first, and then become easily agitated with her and Alex, and then she would spend more and more time holed up in the den, sipping glasses of wine and reading books. They weren't to disturb her during those times. They had both learned that by now.

Once her father would surface, either by phone or in person, it would take a few days for her mother to get back to normal. Diana figured the only reason her mother got a full-time job a year ago was because she was bored playing the waiting game for her father. Things were often tense between the two of them, and though she had never heard loud arguments, sometimes the silence between them was deafening.

She had asked Alex one time if he thought their parents still loved one another. He had told her it was a stupid question, but he hadn't really answered it.

She powered up her laptop, and put on her wireless headset. She went into Creepy Pasta, assuming her handle: D-10. She quickly studied the screen to see who else was in there.

There he was.

Dastardly Damned.

They had met months ago in a Creepy Pasta chat room. An artist after her own heart with his awesome three dimensional sketches of Slender Man and his cohorts which Dastardly Damned had invented straight from his own imagination. She was actually envious of his creativity.

Diana was no slouch at sketching both on paper and online. She even received a great software program called Open Canvas for her last birthday. She used it all the time to put her visions to form, but nothing she had created came close to DD's creations. His were way bolder, more vital, and eye-catching; creatures that only a beautiful mind could create for sure.

Diana sighed and typed a private message.

Hey Dastardly—wanna play?

She waited, but only for a moment, when his reply beeped up on her screen.

Are you sure D10? Aren't you tired of getting your but kicked?

Cocky as always, Diana thought and smiled as she replied with a return message.

I believe there are two t's in BUTT.

His reply came back immediately.

Smart a$$. Let's go in search. Going audio now.

She immediately pulled up their current favorite survival game: *In Search of Slender Man.* She donned her headset with the attached microphone which they both used, when playing interactive. Diana's computer voice sounded like Ariel from *The Little Mermaid.* Dastardly Dan's computer voice sounded similar to Cyborg from *Teen Titans.*

And yes, Dastardly Damned was a pro for sure. He had annihilated her five times in a row, but what he didn't know was that she'd been practicing up on it, and had found a forum where other gamers had shared tricks of the trade for this particular game. She was ready to go to the next level today.

She was ready to take him down.

Four weeks later . . .

This was it. Shit was about to get real. Diana was finally going to meet Dastardly Damned, whose real name she still did not know. But then again, he didn't know hers either. They had agreed not to divulge those until they met in person.

It was Halloween and there was a special costume party to celebrate Diana's favorite holiday. She always loved Halloween. She liked the fact she could assume a costume of any type, and adapt herself to that character. Over her childhood, she'd gone through stages of costume choices. Early on she'd been a princess, Dorothy from the Wizard of Oz, or whatever popular kid's show character of the era. Lame, right?

But for this event, she was determined to have the perfect costume. One that Dastardly Damned most likely would know was her: Slender Man. The whole point of the costume party at the Game Cave was to allow gamers who might not have previously met, to find one another. There would be a contest for best gaming costume, with giveaways for game tokens, and, of course, refreshments would be served. Diana had been so excited about it she'd been working on her costume for weeks.

She was trying to imagine what costume Dastardly Damned would be wearing. He actually had a thing for Bloodborne. Maybe he'd show up as Abhorrent Beast. That would be quite the costume. He also liked Dark Souls and

Final Fantasy. There were a multitude of characters from those games. He had refused to give her any hints whatsoever. There were several main characters in that game. Maybe he would be dressed as Egon or Solaire. Or maybe he'd go with something totally different to throw her off. She smiled at the thought.

Her mother had shown some reservations about her attending the Halloween party, saying she wasn't at all sure going somewhere with everyone in costume at her age might not be the safest thing to do.

She'd finally convinced her mother that at sixteen, she absolutely should have fewer restrictions on her social life. After all, she should be driving at her age the way her parents had allowed Alex to drive at sixteen.

Her mother had finally relented; Diana knew how to spin a guilt trip. The truth was, Diana could have applied for her learner's permit months ago, but she figured why bother since she'd still have to fight with Alex and most likely lose, to get access to the car.

But she had managed to get Alex to drop her off at the Game Cave once she was ready. He was hanging with his best friend, Brian Rutherford, watching college football like they did every Saturday afternoon.

"So," she said, waltzing into the living room where they were both glued to the game, "how do I look?"

She'd taken one of Alex's black dress suits he'd outgrown years ago, put on a white dress shirt, borrowed a black tie from her father's closet, and bought a white nylon knee high stocking to put over her head. She found a man's black top hat at the Goodwill Store which made her costume complete.

"Who the hell are you supposed to be?" Alex asked, shoving a handful of popcorn into his mouth with a smirk.

"Wait, wait," Brian said, "I know who it is. You're the Mummy's Bride!" he announced proudly, giving her a smile and a wink. Her brother burst out laughing and high-fived his buddy.

"Ha, Ha. You're so silly Brian," Diana replied. "I'm Slender *MAN*," she announced giving him an eye roll. " And I'm ready to go to the Game Cave Alex, remember, you said you'd take me?"

"Yeah, yeah," he grumbled. "Can you wait until half time?"

"*Alexxxx*," she whined, "I don't want to be late, c'mon."

"Hey chill there doll," Brian spoke up, "I'll be happy to give you a ride if your lazy ass brother can't tear himself away to give his cute little sister a lift. I gotta be heading home anyway. Hey, heard you have a couple classes with my little brother this year?"

"Thanks, Brian," she replied, "But cute isn't exactly the word I'd use to describe myself, and yes, I have two classes with Danny. He's pretty chill." She felt herself blush underneath the already sweaty nylon head stocking. Danny Rutherford was one of the hot bad boys in her class. Too cool for school, but he'd always been nice to her. He didn't game though, and that was the draw for Diana.

Brian gave her a playful smack, pulling his car keys from his jeans pocket, and held the front door open. "By *cute I* meant without that crazy costume. Aren't there any pretty or sexy game characters you could've gone as? It's a shame to hide such a pretty face and sexy body," he teased as he clicked the remote to unlock the car doors of his newer model Mustang.

"Like who?" Diana asked getting into his car. She doubted very much Brian was into gaming. Alex thought it was a waste of time.

"Well, I think you'd make an awesome Lara Croft. She's pretty hot."

Diana did a double take. "You're actually into Tomb Raider?" she asked, her voice muffled by the stupid stocking she had over her head.

He laughed good-naturedly, "Sure. It's been a while, but hell, it's a classic. And you know, I don't think you're going to be able to do much socializing with that damn stocking stuck over your head. Plus, how are you going to enjoy the refreshments they're serving?"

Diana thought about it. He was right. Dastardly Damned would think she had a speech impediment at the very least, or was hiding a deformed face. It was if Brian had read her mind.

"Hey, I have an idea," he said, as he pulled into the parking lot of the Game Cave and shut off the engine.

He reached into his pocket and pulled out a small pocket knife. "Turn your head and stay still," he instructed. She paused wondering what the hell he planned on doing with that knife. "Trust me," he said chuckling. "I wouldn't dare mar perfection."

She did as instructed, and felt him pull the material from her skin, cutting small slits for her mouth, nose, and eyes.

"There," he said, pulling the visor down so she could see her reflection in the mirror. "Doesn't take away from the Slender Man look, but it has to be way more comfortable, am I right?"

"Yes," she replied, "Thank you, Brian. It is definitely more comfortable."

"So," he continued, "Are you meeting anyone special or going stag?"

Diana giggled. Brian was certainly more interested in her life than her own brother seemed to be. She wondered if it was because he didn't have any sisters. "Why do you ask?" she replied coyly.

"Just curious. You're going into a game room party with people all in costume who you may not know in person. Gotta be careful."

"Actually," she said, "I'm meeting a gaming friend here. A guy actually. We've been playing interactive for months. It's all good. And Alex will be picking me up at eleven."

"Well then you make sure to be careful," he said, reaching across her lap to open the door. "Have fun, Diana. Hope you hit it off with your friend. Be good."

"Gosh," she said with a giggle as she got our of his car, "you're worse than Alex. Thanks for the ride, Brian."

"Anytime, sweetie," he replied with a smile. "Anytime."

It was just after four when she walked through the door of the Game Cave and as she expected, it was packed full of costumed video game characters. The party started at noon and was going until midnight when they closed. She couldn't think of a better way to spend Halloween.

She wasn't sure what time Dastardly Damned would be showing up. He'd messaged her the other day saying he'd be there at some point and would text her when he got there.

She loved the male attention he gave her in his messages. His words made her tummy tingle with something unfamiliar. He was older, he'd admitted that to her. He was eighteen, and she was enthralled with his smoothness; his philosophy on life and on love and seemingly artistic angle to the whole physical aspect of relationships.

He'd shared with her that he'd made love before. Many, many times before. She had read with avid curiosity the details he provided, awestruck at his candidness about it.

She had nothing to share with him relative to her own sexuality. Deep down, she wondered if maybe, just maybe, he could change that for her. In time. Not right away. She wasn't ready to take that step just yet. She knew her brother already had, which in all honesty was to be expected at his age, and the fact that he and Liz were stuck to each other like glue whenever they were together.

Aside from that, Diana had found a half empty box of condoms when she'd been looking around in his desk drawers for some batteries this past summer. She'd never mentioned it to him because he would've chewed her ass for being in his room, not to mention going through his shit. Secondly, it wasn't any of her business and she was glad Alex was mature and responsible enough to practice safe sex.

She was approached by two guys, one dressed as Kratos from God of War, and the other as Ryu from Street Fighters.

"Hey, Slender Man," Kratos greeted, "how's it hanging, dude?"

They both started laughing knowing perfectly well Slender Man didn't have boobs.

"Ha ha," Diana dead-panned. "Hey no shit, you guys did a great job with those costumes. I'm duly impressed."

"I'm Tattered Tank," the guy dressed as Ryu said, "and this is Wretched Wanker201," he finished.

"Nice," she replied, "I've seen you around the chat rooms. I'm Slender Man of course, although my handle is D-10 in the game rooms. Hey, I'm looking for Dastardly Damned, either of you know him from his handle? I've no clue what character he's coming as - most likely one from Bloodborne, but I'm only guessing on that."

They thought for a moment before shaking their heads. "Naw, must be in a different game tribe. We mostly hang with the Black Ops, Dragon Quest, Pillars of Eternity, and of course, our homies here. I haven't seen anyone with that handle in our rooms, have you, Tank?"

"Naw man. Not at all. Haven't seen anyone dressed as a Bloodborne character here, but it's still early. You might want to keep it chill until you get to know this Dastardly Damned better. If you haven't met him yet, you just never know. Some of these gamers can be real creeps - not normal dudes like us, you know?" They both chuckled at the last comment.

Diana nodded in agreement and left to mingle as the size of the crowd was growing by the minute. She knew the guys meant well, but Diana felt like she knew Dastardly Damned as if they had met in person many times before. They shared an online intimacy that few people would understand, but it was special to her.

If only she'd not brushed off Tank's warning she would later think. But his words were too late. Diana was on a collision course with danger. And it would all be evident within a few hours when her limp, bruised, battered, and violated body was found in a wooded area off of Woodley Road. She'd been left for dead and the road ahead for Diana would be a dark, lonely escape from the reality she had no inclination to relive.

Or remember.

But somebody out there remembered well and wasn't about to allow his identity be known if Diana's mental health and stability returned, and that was something he was determined to prevent. His only regret was that he hadn't taken the proper precautions to ensure the body he'd dumped off of Woodley Road hadn't been found until the life had fully drained out of her.

Chapter 1

PRESENT DAY

2 + Years Later

Diana

I moaned against the damp skin of his left shoulder, his kisses felt like fucking, and his fucking felt like a chore I had to endure. I moaned again in feigned pleasure, my voice sounding so damned foreign, even to my own ears. My mind was draped in cognitive dissonance; my thoughts broken pieces of memory and processed responses to his touching, his fucking, his body mating with mine.

Rick or was it Rich? Oh hell, it was one of the two, I just couldn't remember—or maybe I just didn't care. He was here right now. Filling the dark void in my body with his rigid cock; pounding into me with purpose and intent. His pleasure, not mine. That's all men ever wanted from me. To get their pleasure. My fists clenched against his writhing back, my nails dug into his skin, marking him.

"Fuck," he grunted, pumping harder now, "I'm gonna come, baby!"

"Go for it," I groan beneath his weight. "Shoot your load, baby."

And thank fuck he did just that. He pumped ferociously several more times, stiffened and I felt his cock throbbing inside of me, spewing cum inside of the condom I insisted he put on. I might be a dirty whore, but stupid I was not.

It was weird. It seemed like dudes past forty were way more likely to risk catching some STD than guys my own age. But the benefit of fucking older guys was the fact that they didn't mind parting with some money if one was willing to put up with their stamina, no doubt compliments of their little blue pills they carried to cheap motels.

He collapsed against me, his breathing now ragged. "Damn that pussy of yours is tight. Wally gave me a solid when he introduced us, am I right?"

"Oh so, right," I purred, rolling my eyes, my face still buried against his furry chest.

"You didn't come though, did you? This is the third time I've made love to you and you haven't come yet—don't I turn you on, baby?"

Made love?

Is he serious?

"This isn't about my satisfaction, Richard, it's about yours."

"It's Rick," he ground out, rolling off of me onto his back. "I go by Rick, not Richard, and the last name is Mendenhall, remember?"

Well, fuck.

Of course it was. How in the hell did I forget that? Richard Mendenhall. He was one of our county commissioners. His son, Caleb, had been in my class two years ago when I went to Woodrow Wilson High School. He had graduated high school by now. He was probably trying to find his crew at college now; having to start from scratch at an institute of learning that was much larger than the halls of Woodrow Wilson High School to become one of the big men on campus. To ensure that he would not be lost in the crowd, and have an ample number of college coeds drooling to capture his attention.

Back when we were classmates, he had barely acknowledged that I was alive. But the notoriety I'd gained as a result of my much-publicized deadly assault had certainly pivoted me up the ladder of being noticed at school. In fact, it was Caleb Mendenhall who had drummed up the nickname of 'Dirty Diana' I'd then been tagged with once I'd returned to school. That had put him at the top of my list of potential candidates behind the Dastardly Damned handle.

And now I was being paid to fuck his daddy. How rich was that?

"Sorry, Rick," I apologized, "I'm just distracted today I guess. Pre-menstrual."

"Oh baby, it's okay. I get it. Thank God Evelyn is done with all that. Just wish her pussy was as sweet as yours," he said, pulling his tee shirt on over his head. "Say, why don't you go on the pill? Take it straight through. Evelyn used to do that because of PMS. The benefit is no periods. No cramps, no mood swings—"

"No down time from fucking?" I finished, swinging my legs to the floor and capturing my discarded panties.

"Well, you are quickly becoming my favorite vice. Wouldn't mind hooking up more often . . . uh . . . as your schedule permits, that is."

"Can you afford it, Rick? I didn't think county commissioners were paid all that much," I replied, pulling my jeans up over my hips. I turned to gaze over at him. He was forty-six years old. A father. A public figure. And smart enough to know I'd just insulted him. The expression on his face told me everything I needed to know.

"Don't be a bitch, DeeDee. I'm trying to be nice here. You need the money. I need the intimacy."

"Intimacy?" I asked incredulously, "Call it what it is, Rick. You need the *pussy*. The unwrinkled variety, am I right?"

"Don't be vulgar," he snapped, pulling his jacket on and shoving ten twenty dollar bills onto the nightstand next to the bed at the cheap motel where we met to fuck once a week. "It's low class."

I smirked as I pulled my purple sweater over my head. "Rick, this isn't exactly the *Hilton*, dude."

For a moment, I seriously thought I'd pushed a hot button that might set him off into some alternate personality. I enjoyed fucking with clients. It was actually more fulfilling than the sex.

"I'll see you here next Tuesday, DeeDee. Have a great rest of the week."

And then he was out the door of our motel room and I breathed a sigh of relief. I heard the engine of his brand new Charger come to a roar in the parking lot. He wasted no time in putting it in reverse, the tires squealing against the surface of the black top.

He was pissed. But that was on him, not me. For some fucked-up reason, Rich or Rick, wanted to live this fantasy that we were something more than cheating husband and whore-for-hire. Did that make all of this less shameful from his perspective? He didn't even know my real name; didn't know that I had once attended the same high school as his beloved Caleb. His only mention of his son recently was how disappointed he was that the football scholarship he'd counted on to send Caleb to a Big Ten college hadn't panned out. So, poor Caleb was trying to scratch out an identity for his football prowess at the local college.

I wasn't proud of what I did, but it served a purpose so I wasn't ashamed of it either. My circumstances had irrevocably changed over the past couple of years. Most of it, not my fault. At least I didn't see it that way. I had a score to settle, and this was a means to an end. And thankfully, there wouldn't be a next Tuesday for Rick.

I pulled my boots on, checked my watch and saw that I needed to get a move on it if I didn't want to be late to my weekly session with the shrink. I wanted to be done with the psycho-therapy, but I didn't see that happening anytime soon what with the lack of progress I'd made.

In her eyes anyway.

I got into the second-hand car my father had bought me a year ago—no doubt spurned by his own guilt for cheating on my mother and ultimately, leaving us, and heading out to follow the dreams perpetrated by the trauma of my brutal assault—or maybe it was simply an overdue mid-life crisis on his part. Who knows?

I didn't like my sessions with Dr. Addison. But until I graduated high school in a few months, it was a condition of my probation for the crime I'd committed while still under eighteen. It appears I was considered "unbalanced" when I'd been caught shop-lifting a hunting knife from a sporting goods store, and proceeding to slit my wrist with it.

A suicide attempt it was determined. But I'm here to tell you that was false! They didn't understand a damn thing about me.

I was already dead.

Chapter 2

"SO, DIANA, TELL ME how this last week has gone for you?"

"I fucked three guys, Dr. Addison. Still no orgasm," I replied dryly.

She wasn't shocked. She'd heard it a hundred times before.

"You are still using precautions, aren't you?"

I sighed and shifted in my seat. "Yeah, yeah. I'm not *insane*."

"Nobody here thinks you're *insane*, Diana. We all just want you to get better . . . *emotionally*."

Sure you do, Doc.

"How do you find these . . . men?" she asked more out of curiosity than concern.

"Thinking about moonlighting, Doc?" I asked with a smile. "It doesn't pay nearly what you're accustomed to making, trust me."

She gave a slight frown. "No, actually, I'm curious as to how much risk you're taking. Maybe I should notify the authorities. My primary concern has to be your safety."

"Trying to cunt block me, Doc?" I asked, the sarcasm dripping from my words.

She wasn't fazed, but then again, she never was. She always maintained a calm, professional demeanor. Maybe my situation was something she saw on a daily basis. Perhaps I even bored her.

"You need to be kept safe. From men. From yourself," she commented as if it was an afterthought.

No!" I shouted, watching as her head jerked up from where she'd been scribbling notes. "For your information, I've never fucked a stranger, okay? I used to go to school with their kids if you must know. So stay out of my business or I stop talking," I threatened.

She cocked an eyebrow, her eyes squinting as if that would help her determine my honesty. It worked. She showed no emotion to my threat. If I was reading the bitch correctly, she had every intention of carrying through with notifying the authorities. Probably my new school. And then maybe my mother.

"You're sleeping with fathers of your classmates?" she questioned, pen poised awaiting for confirmation.

"Former classmates," I clarified. "And there's just *one* guy at the moment. I dumped the one before him already. Seemed too seedy even for me to be doing two different old men at the same time, but hell, they would've probably loved a threesome. Oh, and for the record, we don't do much sleeping," I finished, feeling foolish that I'd allowed her to intimidate me into the truth.

She was nonplussed. "So, what is the draw for your choices in these men?" she asked.

I wasn't about to divulge my true intentions to her. That would never happen. I shrugged, "The current guy, well I used to go to school with his asshole of a son. Bragged that he was getting a football scholarship to attend some elite college which had a special degree program for Interactive Video Game Development. He used to call me Dirty Diana and thought he was so fucking funny. But guess what? That scholarship never happened. Poor schmuk. Karma really is a beautiful thing, isn't it?"

She scribbled something on her notepad. I could just imagine her note: *Patient shows innate need to seek revenge on popular former classmates.*

"And you mentioned there was another man before the current one Diana?" she prodded.

"Yeah. A guy named Wally. His son, Henry Thompson is a real prick. He acted like he was the king of the gamers back at Woodrow Wilson."

She observed me for a moment. "I'm still not understanding the impetus behind your actions here, Diana. Is it the fact that you don't care for these men's children? Past classmates of yours who did what exactly? I'm trying to understand your motivation here."

"My motivation?" I asked incredulously. "My motivation is to fill the void my father left me with after his desertion with cock. Paternal cock. Sick and depraved? Yeah, I know. But my ultimate goal is to achieve orgasm so I know it's not been a futile journey, got it?" I was so full of shit with that last response that even Dr. Addison had my number on that one.

"You enjoy shocking me."

I had to laugh. Yep, she saw right through it. The truth was that I had my reasons, and they were none of her fucking business.

"If what I say to you is shocking, then your twenty years as a shrink has been totally lame," I finally respond.

"You think so?"

"It doesn't matter to me whether I shock you or not. You set the rules. Truth is to be told in these sessions according to you, well guess what, that's what I've been doing," I lied. "All you seem to do is scribble furiously on your notepad. Never offering insight; never *brainstorming* a solution. That makes you a fraud in my opinion."

"If you're trying to make me angry, it won't work. There's more to your choices of bed partners. It's a pattern. It means something."

"Listen you cunt," I hissed, "I don't give a flying fuck whether you're angry or confused or frustrated or orgasmic. You fucking suck!"

I stood up, grabbed my backpack and prepared to leave in a huff, just like I'd done for the past seven or eight sessions when her steely words stopped me.

"Why don't you talk about the real problem, Diana? Why don't you talk about what *he*, what *Dastardly Damned* did to you . . . that day? Why don't we explore your pattern of behavior since then?"

"That again?" I snarled, walking towards the door of her office. I stopped short of opening it, turned slowly and faced her. I had her full attention. She'd put down her pen, and pushed aside her notebook. We sized one another up, never breaking eye contact. She finally pulled her glasses off, placing them on her closed notebook.

"It's why you're here, Diana. To find some resolution. I don't think we can do that until you talk to me about what happened."

"You've read the police report, the doctor's report, and the witnesses reports. You know as much as I do, Doc."

"That's not true and you know it. You know it, Diana, because you lived it. It was horrific, I get that. It was brutal and savage and incredibly sadistic. But until we discuss it; until we examine how it continues to affect your life, your health, your mind, and the choices you make, you continue to allow him to brutalize you. I'm not sure you get that."

I remained silent for a moment, and then finally sunk back down in the chair I'd just exited. If I didn't play her game, she'd write that down in her weekly report that went straight to my probation officer. Doctor/patient privilege prohibited her from divulging specifics of our conversations, but she was required to report my progress or lack of, as well as if I was being cooperative in the treatment. I was fucked.

"I know you want me to replay that day to you, Doc, but if I can't remember it, then how is that possible?"

She sighed and leaned back in her chair. "I can help you with that. I've explained this to you before. I simply need your permission to put you under hypnosis."

"And then what?" I asked, knowing she'd give me the same spiel she'd given me before but I was determined to put her through the paces anyway. It would burn up some time, and give her the impression I was cooperating by allowing her to discuss it with me again.

"As I explained to you before, hypnosis is a genuine psychological phenomenon that has valid uses in situations where repressed memories exist. It would require several sessions where I attempt to bring you, in a conscious state, to a heightened level of relaxation. Once that is achieved, *if* it is achieved I should say, we then incorporate suggestions through the back door of your consciousness so they take root."

I shifted in my chair. "Bottom line, if this works, what is in it for me, Doc? Do you really want me to relive that day? Why should I even want to?"

"We've been over this. As painful as this might be for you, don't you want to cleanse it from your mind once and for all? To find the perpetrator so that nobody else will have to go through what you went through?"

I shrugged. "Seems to me if the police around here were worth a damn they'd have found the bastard by now. There was enough forensic evidence."

"Yes, but there were no matches in CODIS. That's why this is so important."

"I'll think about it," I replied. "That's the best I can do." Oh, I fully intended to find the perpetrator and then vengeance would be mine.

"You'll let me know next appointment?" she asked pensively. "We need to make better progress in your treatment, Diana."

"Yes," I replied, my voice clipped. "I'll have my answer next appointment. And now I'm heading out to go to home to my lovely halfway house where I can again surround myself with pathetic losers, sacrifice my privacy, and adhere to a curfew that is totally unreasonable. Have a nice day, Doc."

Chapter 3

I'D BEEN LIVING IN a group home or as my probation officer called it: *A Halfway House* for almost a year now, and it beat the hell out of living with my mother. Everything about my life changed that Halloween two years ago, and our family disintegrated for all intents and purposes, one sliver at a time.

For months, I lived in self-imposed silence. I simply didn't want to talk. There was nothing to say. And every time I tried to talk, it encouraged questions I couldn't answer.

Julian Mancini was the only person I talked to at the group home. For some reason his quiet demeanor, and non-intrusive style allowed me to trust him. He knew what I did, but he didn't know what I'd been through. And the fact that he didn't ask is what I appreciated the most about him.

I didn't know a lot about his past, only what he volunteered because intrusiveness worked both ways.

But he had told me that he'd had issues with 'cutting,' which I'd frankly thought was more of a 'girl thing' and kind of blurted that out after he'd shared that with me.

"Nice, Diana," he replied wryly, "Way to be supportive."

"I'm sorry, Julian," I replied softly. "Filtering has always been kind of an issue with me. But hey, I don't judge, so if you want to talk about it, I promise I can disconnect my filter."

And so he had talked to me, and the fact that he'd shared some of the details with me instead of any of the others in the group home, reinforced the feeling that Julian and I would become close friends. And so we had.

Julian came from a large family. One that was wrought with dysfunction in every way imaginable. His father was an alcoholic, and had been physically abusive to the children. He had also molested two of Julian's sisters. Rather than protect her children, his mother had left them to fend for themselves, and after that things had only gotten worse. Julian had run away from home four times by the time he was sixteen. He had gone into the juvenile system, and now at eighteen, almost nineteen, he was at the same place I was: trying to finish high school and become a productive member of society. Just like it was that easy.

As I slammed my backpack down on the couch in the common room, Julian turned from where he apparently was doing homework at the desk.

"Who you trying to impress?" I teased, flopping down on the L-shaped sofa and propping my feet up on the scratched and nicked wooden coffee table.

"Not you," he replied, not even bothering to look up from where he was scribbling answers most likely on the Algebra II sample test which was due tomorrow.

"Can I copy your answers, Julian? I haven't had time to get to my homework assignments yet," I asked him sweetly. Julian wasn't one to deny me anything, which was why I never sweated it when it came to turning in my assignments. We were in every senior class together at Hayward High. I was so glad once I'd gone into the juvenile system two years back that I wasn't in Woodrow Wilson High School's district any longer.

I just wanted to get the hell out of school. I was nineteen now and way past due to be done with school.

"Nope," Julian answered, "You need to do the work, Diana. I'm not going to continue being your crutch. You copy my homework and then flunk the tests, what the hell good does that do, huh?"

Well *this* was new. Julian never got salty with me. I wondered what was up. I looked over at him and saw he wasn't looking at me, though a frown creased his forehead.

"Julian," I said softly, getting up from the sofa and walking over to stand beside the desk, "are you pissed at me for something?"

He sighed, dropped his pencil and ran his hands through his thick, wavy dirty blonde locks. His hair wasn't long on the sides, just on the top. He had that whole *James Dean* look going on, what with the hair, the bluish gray eyes, and the attitude he wore on his facial features which served to give him that brooding appearance which was appealing. I know he turned many of the female heads at school, but he ignored them. He always wore long sleeved tees or jerseys. My guess it was to hide the multiple scars on his arms from years of cutting. I wondered if his legs were scarred as well. Was that typical of cutters? He always wore jeans though so I couldn't be sure.

He turned to me; his tone was that of frustration. "I'm not pissed, Diana, I just think it's time you start to take responsibility for your education. What's your plan? Do you even want to graduate? Or are you gonna settle for fucking old dudes for money and revenge?"

His words clawed at me like a rabid dog. He knew what I did, but he didn't know why, only that I was a broken person who would never again allow myself to be duped by a man.

"I had to see my shrink today if it's any of your business, Julian. She took longer than expected with her ramped up grilling. I don't need *you* judging *me*. I thought we were better than that," I spat, grabbing my backpack and stomping upstairs to my room.

Julian knew that the appointment with my shrink wouldn't have accounted for the amount of time I'd been gone. He would've known I skipped study hall, because we had it together. And yes, I'd confided to him about how I made my money a day or two a week and actually enjoyed fucking the fathers of the dipshits that I hated from Woodrow Wilson High School. I had my reasons.

I'm fucked up! I get it! So does he, so why in the hell is he throwing poison darts at me with his words?

Tears stung my eyes and that wasn't allowed. Tears were a sure sign of weakness, and there was no way in hell I'd ever shed a tear in response to a man's shitty treatment of me. I ran my clothed arm across my face to make them disappear.

There now. I was once again in control of my emotions. That's the way it was supposed to be. Emotions would never cripple me again, punish me for my trust and ignorance, and steal my better judgment.

Then there was a soft tapping on my bedroom door, and Julian's husky voice followed. "Hey, Diana, can I come in?"

"Depends," I called out, sniffling away any remnants of my momentary lapse in controlling my emotions, "if you're going to talk down to me or insult me, just stay on the other side."

"How about if I apologize?" he said, "will that allow me to cross over your threshold fair damsel?"

Now he was being cute. Julian had a natural flair for the dramatic, and with his love of old black and white movies, he used corny language whenever he felt playful or in this case, out of his element. Hurting other people wasn't Julian's thing: he was his own target for that.

"Come on in, fair douche bag!" I called out, sitting cross-legged on my bed.

He came through the door, his brow furrowed in concern. He sat down on the edge of my bed his hands steepled under his chin. "I had no right to act like an asshole downstairs," he said in words not much louder than a whisper. "But dammit, Diana, don't you see what you're doing is every bit as damaging to you as cutting was to me? The only difference is you don't draw blood."

"Oh, so now you're an expert in the field of self-destructive behavior? Is that it? Seems to me you've got more scars than I do," I snapped and immediately regretted it. "I'm sorry," I quickly added, "Now *I'm* being an asshole. It's just that . . . well, Julian, you're the last person I thought would be judgy. You are my only friend, you get that, right?"

"Because we're broken, Diana. And whether we wear our physical scars or emotional ones, it's what we have in common. It's what drew us together."

I thought about his words, and it seemed as if it didn't totally represent our bond. "It's not just that," I replied, "Everyone here is fucked up in some way or the other. Hello? Group home?"

Julian gave me a wry smile and nodded. "Yeah, but they're fucked up for different reasons: drugs, alcohol, petty theft, and worse. We're the only two in here because our family or shrinks thought it was the best course of action. We both come from toxic situations."

I got up from my bed and walked over to where my tablet was lying on the table, and pulled up Spotify. Music was my means of soothing myself. But it wasn't the stuff most people my age liked. I flipped through my playlists and selected The Notting Hillbillies, their lone album: *Missing . . . Presumed Having a Good Time*. The first few chords of "Blues Stay Away From Me" invaded the temporary silence between Julian and me.

"You play that almost every day," Julian commented, coming to stand behind me. "Does it make you feel better to listen to blues and mournful guitars?" he asked.

I turned around to face him, his eyes seemed to have flashed darker, waiting for the answer I didn't have. "Will you show me?" I asked tentatively. He knew what I meant.

"Why?" he asked softly.

"You've seen mine. I want to see yours."

He sighed and brushed a hand through his tousled hair. Then he unbuttoned the cuff on the left sleeve of his plaid flannel shirt and slowly pulled it up past his elbow, exposing his cutting scars to me for the first time.

There were no fresh scars, that much I could tell. I was relieved. They reminded me of slash marks you might see on the top of an old school desk, some of them perpendicular, some of them criss-crossed, some longer than others. All of them were shiny where the scarred skin had heeled up but in a different texture than the unscarred skin. They were lighter and rose up a bit.

I tentatively ran my fingertips over some of them so I could feel the shiny scar tissue. Wondering just how Julian had known not to make them deep enough to require stitches.

"Can I see your other arm?" I asked, still curious as to the extent of his wounds in totality.

"Doesn't look much different," he responded. "Maybe a bit more erratic since I'm right-handed."

"I like erratic," I replied, gazing up at him.

He nodded and proceeded to bare his right arm to me. He was right. The scarring on that one was less patterned. It was helter-skelter. But I touched them because I needed to see if they felt the same as the ones on his left arm. They were a bit more puckered; he'd gone deeper on that arm.

"Do you have scars in other places?" I asked solemnly.

"Wanna find out?" he teased, lowering his sleeves back down and buttoning the cuffs. His eyes were lowered to his task at hand, and I couldn't help noticing how long and thick his eyelashes were.

He was kinda good looking, in a deep, introspective way. I'd never really noticed just how chiseled his features were. Haunting, but not in a bad way. I remained silent to his quip, studying him more carefully. He'd come to the group home about a month after I arrived. But I never really *saw* Julian until now. Not until he bared his scars to me. Why did that make him suddenly look different to me? Different in a good way.

"What?" he asked, now looking at me, "Are you thinking about it?"

I felt my cheeks warm. "You're crass, Julian. We don't roll that way."

He was thoughtful. "Are you disgusted?" he asked pointedly.

"Nope," I replied honestly, "I'm baffled is all."

"Why?"

I shrugged, feeling pressed to give him an honest answer to what was a legitimate question. "It's just . . . I don't understand why you would do that to yourself. I mean, I get that I have a scar on my wrist, but that was purposeful. To end it all," I finished, looking away.

Julian sat back down on my bed, perching his feet on the frame. "You didn't really want to end it Diana, or you would have. It was a cry for help; an attempt to purge yourself of the pain pulsing inside of you same as me. I did mine in small increments, loving the feel of the blood oozing out because with it, my pain dissipated, and nobody had to know. You are a cutter emotionally. You do self-destructive shit to ease your pain without shedding blood. And the difference between you and me is that you're *still* doing it."

I considered his words, and as much as I wanted to, I couldn't dispute the fact that yes, I had wanted the pain to stop, and no, I hadn't wanted to die. I just wanted something or someone to calm the inner turbulence and bitter ache that had taken up residence since Dastardly Damned had taken everything real and normal from me that Halloween night.

But it was still there inside of me. It wouldn't leave and I knew the only way to make it leave was to settle the score. That was my motivation and that was also accountable for my behavior with men. Men of previous fellow students from

Woodrow Wilson High. Because, in my heart, I knew that there was a connection. I hadn't shared that with anyone. And I wasn't sure that I was ready to share it with Julian just yet. But he was right, my emotional cutting wasn't over. But there was a reason for that, and it wasn't something I was ready to share with Julian at the moment.

"Listen," I said, dropping my eyes from his, "I got your point about slacking at school. And yeah, I know what you think about what I'm doing, but you have to trust me, Julian, there *is* a reason for it. I just can't share it with you right now."

His arms were crossed as he let out another sigh. "Whenever you're ready to share your scars with me, I'm here Diana. Now, how about if we cram for that test together? I'll help you but I won't do it for you."

"Sounds fair," I said gracing him with a smile. "Thank you, Julian."

So an hour later, we were curled up on top of my bed, Julian grilling me with practice problems for Algebra II, making me show him my work, and then checking my answers.

"There," he said after checking my last problem. "I think you've got it. See? Not that difficult if you think things through."

"Trust me, Julian. I'm the master of thinking things through."

Chapter 4

JULIAN'S WORDS THE other evening had bothered me more than I had expected. Why had I allowed that exchange between us to seep into a conscience I thought I no longer possessed?

I was too far into my plot of revenge to allow Jiminy Cricket a.k.a. Julian Mancini thwart or stall my mission. If I didn't finish what I started than Dastardly Damned had indeed succeeded in breaking me. And I was too strong to allow that to happen.

The school I now attended was a charter school, and I preferred it that way. No sport teams, no cliques, no familiar faces. But today, it seemed as if the eight periods that comprised it would never end. With each period completed, my pulse had quickened just a bit, knowing there was one less hurdle for me in completing Phase 2 of my master plan.

Phase 1 had taken several months to complete, but the launch, which was Phase 2, would be executed quickly. All those months of having these older men touching me, invading my body, and showing their true black-hearted ways would now come to light for all to see. Let them be judged as harshly as I had been.

I remembered the first day I'd returned to school after my hospitalization. The students and faculty at Woodrow Wilson High had gotten the story - or at least some version of it long before my return. The teachers and administrators treated me as if I were a porcelain doll. One with tiny little surface cracks that needed to be handled with the utmost delicacy, so the cracks wouldn't deepen and suddenly burst into shattered and splintered pieces. They showered me with meek smiles, whispered words of encouragement, and sympathetic nods. It was almost more disturbing than the interactions I'd had with fellow students.

For the first week, my brother insisted on walking me to each and every class, as if he would scare the big, bad, boogey-man away. But his presence by my side hadn't stopped the stares, the whispers, or the kids who looked quickly away as we passed by. They were made uncomfortable by my assault. If they hadn't particularly noticed me before, they sure as hell did now. And it certainly wasn't the type of attention I welcomed. If I'd felt like a misfit before, it was nothing compared to how I felt post-assault.

"Don't worry about them," Alex had told me, "They just don't know what to say or how to react, Diana. It scares them, too."

"How do you know?" I asked him.

"Because," he replied, "What happened to you could've happened to any one of them."

"Not the guys," I countered. "Did you stop to think that the creep who did this to me might be walking down this very hall with us right now?"

Alex had sighed, frustrated that he couldn't make me feel safe even though he wanted to more than anything. "I doubt very much if the monster who did this goes to Woodrow Wilson High. You didn't know his name, or see him, and you told the authorities nothing about him suggested you were even acquainted."

I couldn't deny what my brother was saying, but the fact was, I wasn't about to say anything about Dastardly Damned to the *authorities once I'd re-gained consciousness. How pathetic would that have been? But once I'd returned home from the hospital, two and a half weeks after my "assault," I found that all internet footprints of Dastardly Damned had vanished. Gone. It was if he'd never existed. Just a brutal figment of my deranged imagination.*

I found no trace of him in any of the chat rooms or game groups. My cell phone had not been recovered from the crime scene, and apparently it wasn't 'pinging' off of anything. There was no way I could prove the text messages he'd sent me that evening. It was the first time I'd given him my cell number. I didn't even know his. I'd only given him mine to use if it turned out we couldn't find one another at the Halloween Party, since we were keeping our costumes a secret from one another, or if his plans changed for some reason.

So well-planned it appeared. And when I'd finally come awake from the medically induced coma at the hospital, I'd been forced to deal with the detectives pressing me for information I didn't have, and details I was too ashamed to give. So I answered with one response: "I don't remember."

That hadn't been the truth. How could I tell them all I knew was that I was supposed to meet a guy there named "Dastardly Damned."

"Description?" they'd asked.

"I don't remember. I'm not even sure it was him."

"Why's that?" they'd pressed, their facial expressions not masking their doubt.

"Because we'd never met before. And because I never heard his voice . . . until that night."

They were dubious. As if I wanted to protect the monster. Or perhaps they thought I was afraid he'd come back for me. And I was.

But the truth was I couldn't describe him. What could I have said? Put a BOLO out for a suspect dressed as a Zombie Clown from the video game Left 4 Dead 2?

Yes, my brother had tried his best in the months that followed to be my ardent protector. But it just hadn't been enough.

I shuddered, pushing those memories back into their hiding place in my mind. To be dealt with at another time . . . or maybe never. What was I doing?

But there was no reason not to go forward with my plan. I would flush out Dastardly Damned by process of elimination.

I pulled up the MP3 video uploads on my laptop. "Time to burn you all," I said, an evil chuckle emanating from deep within that actually gave me the creeps. "Pardon the pun."

I opened the package of the new DVD disks, and commenced burning copies for each of my uploaded MP3 videos. I titled them with the name of both the fathers I'd fucked, with the preface "Dirty Deeds." Oh, there had been others, but these two were the top candidates; the fathers of those former classmates at Woodrow Wilson High I suspected of using the cover of Dastardly Damned to destroy me. I'd thought long and hard about who might've hated me enough to want me dead.

And once I'd narrowed it down, it had become my life's mission to have my revenge in a subtle but effective way.

I had approached the men, and made brazen and seductive overtures. It hadn't been difficult to get the first one, Wally. And through word of mouth, I'd then succeeded in getting

Richard Mendenhall on the sheets and secretly videotaped both of them during one of our multiple fuck sessions.

I had positioned my iPhone in such a way that only the men were visible. That hadn't been all that difficult since neither of them wanted to fuck me in any position other than missionary. Talk about boring sex.

But that had been the most important part because very little of me would be visible or identifiable. I selected a couple of the videos to burn, I wanted only the best for my DVD distribution. And once all the DVDs were burned, I would make sure that each of the men, their wives, and their douche-bag sons received them. Because one of those idiots I'd screwed had sired Dastardly Damned. I was sure of it. This operation would hopefully smoke him out.

I inserted an audio dedication at the beginning of only two of the DVDs: those would be the ones sent to each of the two sons using a computer voice, the way Dastardly Damned and I had always done when we gamed on audio together. The message would make sense only to the guilty party.

Message: D10 knows your identity. It's just a matter of time. Final face-off on the horizon. Time to shed your game face.

- Anonymously Yours.

Once finished, I opened my desk drawer, pulling out the padded mailers for the DVDs and addressed them to both of the men at their respective employers' address, the wives at their homes, and to Caleb Mendenhall in care of Woodrow Wilson High School, as well as one to Henry Thompson at the same school. I made sure to mark all of them *Personal & Confidential.* I'd drop them off at the post office tomorrow after school.

I'd just finished up when there was a knock at my door. "Lights out Ms. Webster, it's after ten p.m.," the voice of Edna Banks, our housemother rang out.

I rolled my eyes and turned off my desk lamp. "Got it!" I yelled out. "Good night, Edna."

Tomorrow couldn't come fast enough for me.

Chapter 5

ONE WEEK LATER

I sat across the desk from Dr. Addison once again. I'd pulled a nail file from my backpack, and was filing a snagged fingernail as she settled in, preparing for the barrage of questions, most of which would be repeats of the questions she asked every week. I could hear it now. *"Tell me about your past week, Diana"* was generally the first one. So lame. So boring.

"So, Diana," she said, her pen poised over her notebook, "Tell me how this past week went for you?"

What did I tell you?

"Well, Doc, I think I made a positive behavior change. And it wasn't difficult at all."

"Oh?" she asked, perking up and peering over the top of her readers at me. "Would you care to elaborate?"

No I wouldn't, but yes I will just for you.

"I'm no longer fucking those old men. It's finished. I'm done with it," I replied giving her a rare smile, which I knew she'd find . . . disturbing. I so liked fucking with my shrink. It was the highlight of my week, and how pathetic was that?

She scribbled a note on her pad, nodding and then looked back across her desk at me. "Can you tell me what caused you to take this step? I'm glad of course that you do see it as a positive move as do I, but last week I didn't get the impression you would move in that direction so quickly."

Of course you didn't you frigid ghoul.

"Well," I replied, giving it some faux thought for her benefit, "I guess it was time for me to do some real soul-searching. And that's what I did. I spent the weekend meditating and coming to terms with the present. I realized my self-destructive tendencies weren't worth the pain. So I stopped cutting myself—emotionally I mean." I found Julian's friendship a comforting thing, and his quiet judgment of me was unnerving. I wasn't sure why, but as far as I could tell, his opinion of me was the only one that seemed to matter.

"I can't tell you how pleased I am to hear this, Diana. You are making progress despite your adversity to our counseling sessions." She gave a curt smile as if she had somehow gotten one over on me and was proud of herself.

"So, tell me, how are things going in the group home? Have you cultivated any friendships?"

"One," I answered honestly. "A guy at the group home. His name is Julian and well . . . we have a lot in common."

"How so?" she asked, busy scribbling down her notes.

"We've both been tossed away by our families. We both used different methods to cope with our pain I guess. He's quiet. And reflective."

"So, is your friendship with this Julian of the platonic nature?"

Of course you would ask that.

"For now," I replied, blowing the nail dust away from my cuticles.

"I just caution you Diana to take things slow. Oftentimes, we've a tendency to skew the boundaries between friendships and romance."

"Oh, do you do that Dr. Addison?" I asked cockily, "Because none of my past sexual relationships have involved either friendship or romance. More of just raw revenge fucking for the hell of it. Know what I mean?"

I could see her face tighten at my vulgarity. She really needed to loosen up and at least make an attempt to act shock-proof if she was ever going to be worth a damn as a therapist. At least that was my opinion.

"No need to dwell on the past demons, Diana. I think you are making a great effort to shed those moving forward. However, I must be honest that I still have concerns that something could trigger you back to that destructive path you were on which is why I'm interested in the interactions between you and this Julian."

"No worries, Doc. I finalized the official ending of that destructive path by mailing out the DVD's of my fuck sessions with those dirty men to their significant others. I titled the disks: *Dirty Deeds*. Fitting, right?" I laughed as I relayed this to her, wondering what the various reactions had been upon opening the padded envelopes I mailed out last week. I would give anything to be a fly on the wall to watch the looks of horror appear on their respective faces when they viewed them.

More importantly, I was waiting to see which one flushed out Dastardly Damned. It seemed to me he'd be making some noise soon. I had my senses on high alert and was careful to never leave the group home without protection. Any by that, I wasn't referring to condoms.

"What prompted you to do such a thing, Diana?" My shrink was asking this question as if she didn't possess one iota of knowledge about how I rolled or what made me tick. Such a waste of money this one.

I yawned and stretched out my arms, rolling my neck from side to side until it cracked so I could once again relax. "Why don't you tell me. You're the shrink, right?"

"I think perhaps we need to deal with these issues in more depth next week. I think you are motivated by something more than what you've divulged thus far. I would really like to give the hypnosis a shot. The timing is right for it."

I got up from where I was sitting, and pulled my jacket on. "We'll see," I said. "Maybe."

"I really think it would be a major breakthrough for you, Diana. Please give it some thought."

"See you next week, Doc."

On the way back to the group home, I actually gave some thought to Dr. Addison's multiple suggestions that I undergo hypnotic therapy. I'd resisted it from the start. At first I did it simply because it was a control thing. I resented having to see a shrink, so I was determined to make our sessions as miserable for her as they were for me.

I found perverse pleasure in my attempts to shock her with my scathing revelations; my vulgar confessions. My total dismissive attitude towards her very profession served to feed her need to put me under this hypnosis kick she was on. So, by being obstinate and uncooperative on the whole topic allowed me to control the narrative - or so I'd thought.

But now I realized that it had more to do with fear than control. Maybe the truth was that I was afraid hypnotherapy would reveal more than what I was prepared to know. Perhaps it would unleash details of that night I wasn't prepared to handle.

But what could be worse than what I'd been through since then? This was the question that kept nagging at me. Despite the fact I had narrowed the field down to two individuals who were top contenders for Dastardly Damned, why had I been so reluctant to at least give the hypnotherapy a shot, if for no other reason than it just might confirm one over the other?

I didn't want to relive that night. But hadn't I been reliving the effects of that night ever since?

It was a confusing situation for me. Maybe I should approach Julian with it. He'd earned a little bit of my trust - more so than anyone else still active in my life. What did I have to lose?

Chapter 6

"HYPNOTHERAPY?" JULIAN asked, running his hands through his thick wavy hair. The sleeve of his sweater drooped slightly, exposing one of the crisscrossing scars on his wrist. I had to fight the urge to reach out and touch it. "Does it even work?"

"Hell if I know," I replied dryly, My shrink says it will. But she says a lot of things."

"But if it does you'll remember? You'll know who attacked you?" Julian asked. He took a seat beside me on the moth-eaten couch. His voice was low and his brows furrowed. The tiny common room was empty except for us and the only other sound was the drone of the television which was on the local news channel.

"Maybe..." I said, avoiding the penetrating gaze of his steely blue-grey eyes, "But do I want to remember? I blocked it out for a reason, right? Maybe it's best if I never relive that awful night."

Julian was silent for a moment, nodding. Of anyone, he should be able to understand that some things were better left forgotten. I was sure he had his share of memories he'd rather not relive.

"But can you live without knowing?" he finally asked. I dared to meet his gaze. The truth was, I couldn't. However, what Julian didn't know was that I had a plan. I bit my lower lip, weighing the idea of telling him everything but decided against it. His judgmental words from the other day still stung and if he were to admonish me like Dr. Addison, I might not be able to handle it. For some reason his approval of me was important. It mattered and I wasn't sure why.

I realized I'd been quiet for a long time. Julian was still staring at me expectantly.

"I don't know, okay?" I huffed. "I just don't know what to do. What I do know, though, is that I sure don't want to give my cunt doctor the satisfaction of convincing me of anything."

Julian smirked. "That sounds about right," he replied. "You control the information coming in and going out."

Silence fell again and our eyes drifted towards the TV. A reporter with painfully thin eyebrows and large, perky tits was interviewing a local farmer about his prize-winning potato. I couldn't help but roll my eyes at the asinine segment. I turned my gaze back to Julian, who seemed to be watching it with some shadow of amusement. I cleared my throat.

"Hey Julian, I stopped fucking old guys for money," I said casually, smiling as I watched Julian's eyes go wide, as once again I had his full attention. Suddenly he'd forgotten the farmer and his ten-pound potato.

"That's... good," he replied. The hint of a smile played on his lips and it mirrored my own. "I'm, proud of you. So, who are you fucking now?" he asked quirking a brow.

"Currently? No one," I responded, surveying my cuticles aloofly, "Why? Are you interested in the position?"

Julian's eyes flashed with devious passion for a fleeting moment. Then he shook his head and looked away. "I thought you said it wasn't like that between us."

"It's not," I responded quickly. He nodded, and then turned those steely eyes back on me.

"But I have to wonder. Did they please you?" he asked, "Those men. Did they please you?"

His directness startled me momentarily. It was a question I was surprised he would ask. I wasn't sure how to respond.

"Sure," I lied, unconvincingly. Julian raised an eyebrow at me.

"What I mean is that it felt good to get fucked. To feel alive and in control. To fill that dark void inside of me."

"But *was* it good? Was it passionate?" he persisted, obviously on his own mission to dissect my psyche.

I suddenly recalled being in a cheap motel bed with Rick, my face hidden in his hairy chest so he couldn't see the bored expression on my face while he continued to thrust his mediocre cock in and out of me like a lifeless robot. Or Wally, who could hardly last five minutes and tried more than once to secretly slip the condom off before we did the deed. I chuckled joylessly to myself.

"No, it was far from romantic."

"Did you come?" Julian asked, his gaze unwavering. I felt myself flush slightly. I was used to being the crass one, the one who spoke unflinchingly and fucked indiscriminately, but for some reason talking about the intimate details of my sordid sex life felt different with Julian. I swallowed hard and shook my head no.

"No one has ever made me come," I replied softly. Julian's face twitched with suppressed shock.

I suddenly felt incredibly exposed. I couldn't help but wonder if this is how he felt when he showed me his scars.

"Well," he said, his voice even softer than mine, "I think you deserve to be with someone who will please you. Who will make you come. Who will make love to you, not just fuck you and leave the money on the nightstand."

I bristled slightly at his words, overwhelmed by the intensity of the moment. My heartbeat was fast and hard.

"I made my choices," I replied firmly. "Good or bad, they were mine and now I'm done with those men."

"It's not too late to make different ones," Julian said. I suddenly became aware of how close our bodies were on the tiny couch. My face was hot and I struggled to find the words to snap back at him. I couldn't think about anything besides how long and thick his eyelashes were. The moment was interrupted, though, when something on the news caught my attention.

I pulled away from Julian, breaking the tension that pulsed between us. On the TV, the same well-endowed reporter had just announced breaking news. It was the name she said, though, that stole my focus. My already pounding heartbeat doubled in speed as I read the scrolling banner that flashed across the bottom of the screen.

County Commissioner Caught in Sex Scandal

My blood ran cold and I leaned in, my ears now tuned to every word.

"This evening, a sex tape surfaced featuring none other than Athens County Commissioner, Richard Mendenhall. Though the clips show only partial parts of the female in the video, she has yet to be identified. However, we have confirmed that the mystery woman is *not* the

Commissioner's wife, and have reason to believe that the woman was a sex worker."

To my horror, a still frame from my iPhone sex tape suddenly appeared in bright pixels before my eyes. Thanks to my strategic camera angles, my face didn't make the shot, and any of Mendenhall's body parts that rated higher than PG-13 had been obscured by thick black bars. All that could be seen of me was a small section of my slight frame. A bent leg, a flat naval, a forearm with a crappy stick-and-poke tattoo of a dagger that I'd let a pot dealer at a party give me after one too many PBR's a year ago. Hovering above me was Rick, caught in a moment of utterly embarrassing ecstasy, his head tilted back so that his face was clearly identifiable. Mercifully, the image disappeared and the serious face of the reporter returned.

"We've reached out to Commissioner Mendenhall for a comment on the scandal but he has refused to break his silence. However, his wife, Donna Mendenhall, has let us know that she is devastated by the revelation and has made plans to file for divorce. Mr. Mendenhall will be brought before the Ethics Committee tomorrow and is expected to tender his resignation. We'll keep you updated as the events unfold. This is Melanie Montero for Local Five and we'll be right back after this short commercial break. Stay with us."

I felt my blood freeze solid - like ice on a pond, and my thoughts begin to swirl like a vortex. Well, the cat was certainly out of the bag now. Questions raced through my mind. Who would have leaked the tape? And why? I was so preoccupied with my own panic that I hardly noticed Julian staring at me, assessing my face. My shock and confusion was certainly written all over it.

"No..." he said. It was somewhere between a question and an accusation. I swallowed hard and shrugged. "That's not *you*, is it?"

"Busted," I said, my voice hollow.

"Jesus Christ, Diana," he snapped, suddenly getting to his feet. His look of disdain cut through me like a knife, going straight to my core. "You do realize you ruined that man's life, don't you?"

My confusion turned quickly to anger.

"Me?" I asked incredulously. "I didn't make him go to that motel with me. I didn't make him cheat on his wife. And I sure as hell didn't send that video to the fucking local news."

"But you made that video," Julian countered, "and if you didn't send it to the station, someone else did, which means you sent it to *someone*."

"Yeah," I snapped, jumping to my feet, my rage white hot, "I sent the video to him and his wife and his piece of shit son and *maybe* if you weren't acting like such a judgmental dick I'd explain why. It's complicated. Very complicated, okay?"

"It's *always* complicated with you, Diana," Julian said, shaking his head. He made no attempt to hide his disgust. He took a deep breath in and blew it out, tipping his head back to stare at the water-stained ceiling of the halfway house we called home.

"Listen," he finally said, "there's an algebra test tomorrow and I need to study. I'll see you later, okay?"

"I thought we were going to study together," I mumbled, but it was too late. Julian was already stalking off toward his bedroom, leaving me alone to listen to the peppy cereal commercial that blared from the TV. The optimistic jingle made me want to put my fist through the screen.

With a huff, I collapsed back into the musty couch and tried to slow my racing thoughts. I should have predicted something like this. Dirty secrets like these always had a way of coming to light.

Now if only the same could be said for the secrets I'd actually like to know. I pulled my legs up on the couch and put my head between my knees.

One thing, at least, was for certain. If there was any chance that Caleb Mendenhall was Dastardly Damned, I was on his radar once again. Fortunately, this time, he was also on mine.

ANDREA SMITH

Chapter 7

DESPITE HAVING EVERY class together, Julian hardly spoke a word to me the next day. I couldn't find him in our usual lunch spot, the school auditorium, which was always empty except for us.

We liked to sit in there, picking at our food, listening to our voices echo. That day, however, I ate lunch alone. In algebra class, he even sat across the room from me rather than right in front, where I could peek over at his paper when I struggled with an answer.

Despite the help he'd given me a few days prior, I'd spent the previous evening distracting myself from disaster with a horror movie marathon and the result was that I was sleep-deprived, unprepared, and incredibly jumpy. I'd be lucky to scrape by with a C- and graduation was looking more and more like an impossible fantasy. By the time the last bell rang, I was cranky, red-eyed, and exhausted.

I scanned the crowd of buzzing students for Julian as we exited the building in a flood of bodies.

He was nowhere to be found. I wondered how long it would be before he forgave me, and then found myself getting angry that I felt the need to apologize at all. What had I done to wrong him?

Nothing. If he was going to judge me, like everyone else, then fuck him. He wasn't the friend I thought he was in the first place. Still, as I pushed through the back door and headed toward my car, I kept an eye out for Julian's beater. Maybe that's why I didn't notice the angry man making a beeline straight for me. It wasn't until his hulking frame blocked the sun from my eyes that I looked up and to my dismay, was greeted by a familiar face.

It had been more than two years since I'd last seen him. He'd grown taller and his hair was already beginning to thin, even at his tender age. I hadn't known back when I attended Woodrow Wilson High School that he was the spitting image of his father. Of course, I knew that now. In fact, I knew his father well. Our sex tape scandal was splashed across the cover of the daily paper.

That's because the person standing before me was Caleb Mendenhall, and he was angry.

"I need to talk to you," he growled.

I was so taken aback by his sudden appearance that I stumbled and nearly fell flat on my face.

The realization hit me like a Mack truck; I could be looking Dastardly Damned right in the face.

"What are you doing here?" I asked, my eyes darting around at the quickly-emptying parking lot.

Only a few students lingered by their cars, chatting with one another, oblivious of the confrontation occurring a mere few feet away. Meanwhile, the rest of my peers couldn't get off school grounds fast enough.

"What are you doing *fucking my father*?" Caleb asked. His voice was steady but his eyes flared with unbridled anger.

"I don't know what you're talking about," I snapped, sidestepping him in an attempt to make it past him to my car.

He quickly stepped back in front of me, though, blocking the way.

"I know that was you in the video, Dirty Diana."

I clenched my fist at the mention of that cruel nickname. He'd been the one to coin it, right after the attack. He wasn't the only one who seemed to lack sympathy for me. Plenty of kids whispered nasty things behind my back. They said that I was asking for it, or that I had made it all up to get attention, or that I must have been drunk or high as if that should matter. Caleb, though, had stood apart in his cruelty. It's what had made me suspect him in the first place.

"You don't know shit," I spat, trying to sidestep him again. Once more, he blocked my way. He pointed to my forearm, where my rolled-up sleeve exposed a crooked stick-and-poke tattoo.

"I recognized that ugly ass tattoo. You might not post any selfies on social media anymore, but there's still a picture of *that* on your Instagram profile. I wasn't sure where I recognized it from at first, but there's no mistaking it now. You're the whore from that disgusting video."

His voice was increasing in volume and his hands had begun to shake. Caleb was getting angrier by the second but still, none of the parking lot stragglers seemed to notice. I gripped my keys tightly in my fist, ready to jab them into his face if he came too close. I took a step back and gathered al my guile.

"Why do *you* think I fucked your father, Caleb?" I asked, daring him to confirm my suspicions.

"Because you're a fucking slut," he yelled back. The hair on my arms stood up. His hands were balled into fists and his knuckles were white.

"My dad's going to lose his job. The story is everywhere. My parents are getting a divorce - and it's all because of you."

"Your parents are getting a divorce because your dad couldn't keep his tiny dick in his pants," I snapped. For a moment, I was afraid Caleb would hit me. He took a step forward and I braced for impact. Instead, though, his anger suddenly became tinged with something else. For a second he looked as if he was holding back tears.

"I just want to know why. Why him? Why did you have to ruin *my* family?"

The question sent a fresh surge of emotions coursing through me. In a moment of confidence, I stepped forward, my eyes narrowed.

"I don't know, Caleb," I replied in a quaking whisper. "Why you? Huh? Could it be because I wanted revenge? Because I wanted to get back at you?"

"Revenge?" he asked incredulously, his glassy eyes drying instantly and his brows furrowing with anger once again. "Why would you want revenge on me?"

I didn't say a word. Just stared long and hard at his contorted face. *Admit it,* I silently demanded.

Admit what you did to me.

"Wait," Caleb said, taking his own step backward, "Is this because of that stupid nickname? Is that why you did all of this? Because I was mean to you in high school?"

I let out a manic laugh. The sound was unfamiliar in my ears.

"A nickname?" I shouted. "No, no, no. It's way bigger than that."

My entire body began to shake. A combination of panic and rage pumped through my veins like poison. I suddenly realized that the parking lot had cleared. I was alone with the man that well might be Dastardly Damned. I felt bile rise in my throat and I gripped my keys tighter. I gulped and quickly darted past Caleb, making a break for my car. I made it only a step past him when I felt a hand wrap around my wrist and tug hard. My backpack slid off my shoulder and hit the ground with a thud as Caleb whipped me around to face him.

In that moment, I wouldn't have hesitated to stab him right in the face with the sharp end of my car key; or gouge out his dark and menacing eyes, but his death grip on my arm made it impossible. Bile crept further up my throat and I thought for a moment that I might be sick.

"What the fuck is wrong with you?" he shouted, shaking my arm so violently I nearly lost my balance again. I tried to pull away but he held on. His clasp was so tight it hurt and my hand started to go numb. I looked around wildly, wondering if I screamed for help, would there be anyone to hear?

"You owe me an explanation," he shouted again, louder this time. My vision started to narrow with panic.

"I owe you nothing, you fucking monster," I shouted back. In a sudden burst of movement, I twisted my arm around, loosening his clutch just enough to pull myself free. Without a second thought, I shoved my knee in the direction of his groin, hoping to bring him to his knees so I could make my escape. Caleb dodged just in time, and my leg missed his squishy bits, connecting instead with his upper thigh.

"Shit," I whispered to myself.

He stumbled back but recovered quickly. More quickly than I was able to make it to my car. I took a deep breath in as his eyes glowed nearly red with fury. I braced for impact once again as he lunged toward me, hands outstretched, but as if stopped short by an invisible force, he only swiped uselessly at the air, somehow unable to come closer. He spun around in shock and it was then that I saw what prevented him from reaching me.

Behind him, Julian stood, one arm outstretched and a handful of Caleb's sweatshirt grasped in his fist. As Caleb turned, Julian cocked his fist and swung, hitting him squarely in the eye with a mean and very impressive left hook. Caleb cried out in pain and stumbled back. Before he could get his bearings, Julian hit him again, sending him to his knees.

"Stay the hell away from her, you hear me?" he snarled.

Caleb scrambled to his feet and swung wildly in Julian's direction. Julian was smaller and lighter than the ex-football player but he was quicker, too. And with the element of surprise on his side he clearly had the upper hand. He dodged the blow with ease and shoved Caleb back down to the ground.

"Get in the car, Diana," he yelled. I suddenly realized I'd been frozen in place. I grabbed my backpack from the ground and sprinted the remaining ten feet to my car, floundering to get the key in the lock. I heard the sound of flesh and bone colliding behind me and turned just in time to see Caleb land his first punch. Julian let out a small sound of pain but dodged the second blow just in time.

"GO!" he yelled at me. Fighting my instinct to turn back and help him, I swung open the car door and threw myself inside. Seeming satisfied that I was safe, Julian began to back away from an advancing Caleb. In an instant, he'd pushed past Caleb's hulking frame and slipped into his own car, locking the door behind him just as Caleb pulled against the door handle.

"Fuck you!" he screamed, banging his rapidly bruising fist on the windshield, "You're gonna pay, you hear me? You're gonna pay!"

I didn't wait another moment. I jammed the key into the ignition and turned it, feeling my old car sputter to life beneath me. I rammed the gear shift into reverse and peeled out of the spot, accelerating out of the parking lot as fast as possible with Julian on my heels. As the tires kicked up gravel, I looked in the rearview mirror only once, catching a final look at Caleb Mendenhall as he kicked the ground in frustration.

Chapter 8

I HAD ALMOST STOPPED shaking by the time I reached the halfway house and parked my car in the lot outside. I took a deep breath to steady myself and put my feverish head on the wheel.

That had certainly been an unexpected encounter. And strangely enough, there was a good chance I'd just come face to face with my monster. Caleb didn't seem to know what I was talking about, why I might want to have my revenge on him, but who's to say that wasn't just his game? Still, I couldn't forget the look of bewilderment on his ugly face. The whole ordeal had left me feeling even more confused than before.

When my breathing returned to normal, I grabbed my backpack from the passenger seat and climbed out of my car, scanning the lot for Julian. He'd been behind me the entire way there but must have turned off at the last second. There was no sign of his or his hunter-green Volvo. The unfamiliar feeling of guilt nagged at the back of my mind. He was probably pissed at me. I guess he deserved to be, this time. With a sigh, I locked my car and made my way toward the front door, my mind still a swirling mass of madness.

The first thing I saw when I stepped inside was the solemn face of our housemother, Edna. Her mouth was a tight, straight line, and there were lines of concern etched deep into her forehead.

She was seated in her favorite armchair in the common room, reading a dusty hardcover book, but she dog-eared her page and set it aside when she caught sight of me.

I tried to escape to my room, shooting her a half wave, but she gestured for me to stop.

"Wait up, Diana," she said, slowly climbing to her feet and crossing her arms across her chest.

"Can this wait?" I asked curtly. "I've had one hell of a day and I'd really just like to get some sleep."

"I'm afraid not," she replied, her tone stern. "You need to come with me."

I rolled my eyes but followed her through the common room into her tiny office. Stacks of files, one for every member of the house, were neatly placed on her desk beneath a series of cheesy, inspirational posters.

It always seems impossible until it's done.
Out of a mountain of despair, a stone of hope.
Every day is a chance to be better.

The empty promises of some sort of shining future gave me hives. I tried to avoid looking up at them, or into Edna's concerned face, as I took a seat in a folding chair beside her desk. Edna sat as well and opened the first drawer. She pulled out a piece of paper and smoothed it out, then turned her focus on me.

"When I arrived here this afternoon, after doing some grocery shopping to restock the communal pantry, I found something alarming. It was a note, addressed to you. It was tacked up on the door. With a knife. And the content is... *alarming.*"

For the second time that day, I felt my heart skip a beat in fear. I sat in silence, unsure of what to say.

"Can you tell me why someone would do something like this?" Edna asked. She was working hard to maintain the calm, soothing voice she always spoke in, but it was clear that she was deeply concerned. The looks she gave me reminded me of my teachers back at Woodrow Wilson. The way they stared down at me with a mix of worry and pity, tinged with disgust. It made me irrationally angry.

"Well, it would help if I knew what the hell you were talking about," I quipped, cocking my head to the side defensively. Edna sighed and slipped off her glasses, taking a painstakingly long time to wipe the smudges away, before finally pushing the letter across the desk to me. I held my breath as I read it.

Diana,

It's you in the video. Caleb knows too. Surprise, we talk, still.

Soon, everyone will know what you did, unless you leave my family the hell alone. I don't know what sick shit you've gotten into, but if you come anywhere near my father ever again, I'll end you. I know where you live. I know where you go to school. I can find you, wherever you go.

This is your only warning.

- H

I read the note twice, struggling through the messy scrawl, then pushed the paper back towards Edna.

"I have no idea what this means," I lied. Edna stared back at me, unblinking.

"Diana," she said gently, "Are you sure?"

"Yeah, I'm fucking sure," I snapped. Edna's already pursed lips nearly disappeared.

She folded the note back up and slipped it back inside the drawer with a slow exhale.

"Be that as it may, the contents of this letter are still incredibly disturbing. Furthermore, the nature of the threats makes me concerned for your safety and the safety of the other residents at this facility."

"It's probably nothing," I said, with a dismissive wave of my hand, "Some sort of weird prank by some kids."

"That's possible," Edna replied, nodding her head slowly, "But I still think it's best if you speak to the police."

"No," I said quickly. Memories of police interviews flashed back to me. Being asked the same questions over and over by toad-faced cops as I sat in the hospital bed, the beeping of my heart monitor counting off the endless seconds. Talking to the police was the last thing I wanted to do, especially when it meant revealing my identity as the mystery whore who banged the county commissioner. There was no damn way.

"I'm afraid it's non-negotiable," Edna said firmly. "It doesn't have to be today, but you'll need to inform them of this eventually. Whether or not it's a prank, the author of this note has threatened you directly."

"What if I say no?" I asked, crossing my arms across my chest and leaning back in my chair indignantly.

"Well," Edna said, the melodic quality of her voice evaporating, "I'm afraid that you won't be able to stay here if your presence could mean danger for the other residents. I'm responsible for securing everyone's safety who resides here."

"And where would I go?" I asked, alarmed by the panic in my own voice. I was never scared, only angry, but now I was beginning to feel fear creep over me.

So far, my master plan had brought me no closer to DastardlyDamned. If anything, I realized with a sinking feeling, it had only put a target on my back. It had seemed like such an act of nefarious genius in my head, but in the few days since I'd sent those DVDs, things had only become more complicated. Here I sat, now at risk of being booted from the group home. Would that mean I would be sent to jail for some sort of probation violation? And what about Julian? A wave of nausea washed over me like a rolling tide. I felt light-headed and nearly doubled over.

"Fine," I spat. "I'll talk to the damn cops if that's what it takes. Just don't kick me out, okay? I don't have anywhere else to go."

Edna's face softened.

"I'll give you some time but not much," she said. "I'm very sorry about this, Diana. I know it must be very frightening."

She put her hand gently on my shoulder and gave it a comforting squeeze, but I quickly pulled away. It was strange. I didn't mind letting strange men inside of me, but something about a gentle and comforting touch made me recoil.

"Can I go?" I grunted. Edna nodded.

"Please keep me updated," she said. "In the meantime, I've arranged for extra security. You can sleep soundly tonight."

"Yeah, right," I mumbled as I gathered my things and made my escape. The poor old bat didn't know the half of it.

When I passed by Julian's room on the way back to my own, I noticed his door was ajar. I paused and knocked gently, allowing it to swing open, revealing Julian lying on his threadbare blanket strumming an out-of-tune guitar he'd gotten at a garage sale the month before. When he saw me in the doorway he abandoned his attempt at a 'C' chord and set the instrument aside. A fresh bruise throbbed above his left eye.

"That looks like it hurts," I said as I drifted into his room and took a seat at the foot of his bed. "You should probably put an ice-pack on it to help keep the swelling down."

"Yeah, I'm good. You should see the other guy," he replied with a wry chuckle. He paused for a moment, searching my worried face for the answer to a question he was yet to ask.

"You want to tell me what that was all about earlier?" he finally asked.

"Do I want to?" I asked, lying back on the bed, stretching out across it horizontally, and staring at the cracked paint on the ceiling. "Well no, I don't, but I guess you deserve to know. But I swear, if I see one hint of judgment on your face or in your body language, I'm shutting up and maybe bruising that other eye, too."

"That's fair," Julian said. He shimmied down and lay beside me, staring up at the same spider web of chipped plaster. I squeezed my eyes shut and after taking a moment to collect my thoughts, I began to speak.

I told Julian everything. I told him about my plan with the videos, about my suspicions of Caleb and Henry. I told him about the men I slept with and their shithead sons, how they'd been unflinchingly cruel to me at my very lowest. I told him about the threatening letter and my conversation with Edna. I told him about the man I met online, Dastardly Damned, who I was supposed to meet up with on that fateful Halloween night, and how I wanted to lure him out from hiding and find out who it was that brutalized me, once and for all. Julian listened, silently, his expression blank, until I finally finished my story and lay breathless beside him, feeling drained and empty.

"Well fuck, Diana," he finally said. The simplicity of his response made me laugh in spite of myself.

"Tell me about it," I replied.

"Listen, I swear I'm not judging you, but damn, in all seriousness that was a stupid plan."

"You wouldn't be saying that if it had worked," I retorted defensively.

"Well , if it had worked, it wouldn't have been a stupid plan," Julian shot back. "But it didn't and it put you in danger." I didn't have much of a comeback for that because he was right.

"So, what are you going to do?" he asked, sitting up and running his hands through his messy hair. Julian always did that when he was stressed or perplexed. I knew him well enough by now to read his every move.

"I wish I knew," I said glumly, lifting myself up onto my elbow to meet his gaze.

"Do you think either of these guys could be your attacker?" he asked. "Is one of them Dastardly Damned?"

"I don't know," I said, shaking my head. Hair fell in my face but I didn't bother to flick it away. Bright purple obscured half my vision. It wasn't the sickly, gray-purple that I used to wear back at Woodrow Wilson High School. It was shockingly violet, bright, and alarming like the coloring of a poisonous Amazonian creature, a warning to anyone who looked at me to stay back.

I broke the momentary silence. "I think it's clear who wrote that note. The only person that makes sense for it was Henry. The second of my two top suspects. And you saw Caleb in the parking lot at school today. Both of them are filled with so much *rage*. I just can't tell if it's *'you fucked my dad'* rage or *'you were supposed to die alone in the woods off a dead-end road'* rage. Either way, they're pissed, and they know where to find me if they want to make me pay. This entire thing has turned into an absolute disaster."

Julian nodded his head. I searched his features for any sign of judgment, but more than anything, he looked pained. Without warning, he suddenly leaned over and kissed me.

I was so shocked I couldn't react. I didn't pull away or kiss him back. I just lay there, eyes open wide, frozen in shock. Before I could even process what was happening I heard someone clearing their throat, pointedly, behind me. Julian pulled away and I spun around to see Edna glaring straight at me. Well, damn.

"It's time for lights out," Edna said, her voice icy. I cursed under my breath and got to my feet as Julian looked away sheepishly.

"Not so fast," Edna snapped, putting up her hand and blocking the door frame. "Evidently, I must remind you of our policy about resident relationships, which of course, are expressly forbidden. If I see you two engaged in any sort of romantic affection again, you both will be removed from this house, do you understand me?"

"I'm sorry," Julian mumbled, "It's not her fault, it was me, I kiss-"

Edna cut him off.

"This is your only warning," she said, "And Diana, you especially are on thin ice. Now get to bed." She stepped aside and I shuffled out of the room, not daring to look over my shoulder as I did.

Of all the strange things that happened today, Julian's kiss was certainly the least expected.

Even as I stumbled into my room, clicked off the lights, and crawled into bed still fully dressed, I couldn't forget the sensation of his lips on mine. I closed my eyes, head spinning, and let exhaustion consume me. That night I dreamed of Dastardly Damned. He loomed, faceless, above my bed, taunting me with his hidden identity. When I woke up the next morning, the solution was painfully clear. There was only one way to be entirely sure which of the two boys was the one who stole my life away. I needed to remember. I would have to let myself be hypnotized.

Chapter 9

I WANTED TO KNOCK THE smug smile off Dr. Addison's face. She was altogether too pleased with herself upon hearing my request, no doubt believing my change of heart was due to her miraculous abilities as a therapist.

As if.

I sunk low in my seat and glowered as she scribbled something onto her notepad before responding.

"So, what brought about this sudden shift?" she asked, leaning forward in her chair and observing me like a zoo animal in a cage. I fought the urge to roll my eyes back in my head, or even better, to storm out in my usual way.

"I need answers," I responded flatly.

"Do you think you're mentally prepared to remember your attack?" Dr. Addison asked, tapping her pen against the pad thoughtfully.

"I dunno Doc," I replied, "Isn't it your job to decide that? If you thought I wasn't ready, why have you been trying to convince me to do this shit for months?"

"I didn't say that *I* didn't think you were ready," Dr. Addison explained, "I'm simply asking if *you* think you're ready."

I sighed and rubbed my itchy eyes. I was coming off two nights of bad sleep and it was beginning to take its toll. My reflection in the mirror above Dr. Addison's desk proved it. I looked haggard. My eyes were ringed with puffy blue bags and my vibrant hair was piled, unwashed, atop my head in a messy bun. I could hardly stand to look at myself.

"I'm as ready as I'll ever be," I said honestly. "I don't think things could get any worse inside my head as they are now. I have to take a chance if I ever want to feel in control of my life or my future again."

That seemed to be enough for Dr. Addison. For the first time ever, she set her pen and pad to the side, stood, and crossed to her desk where she flicked an old-fashioned metronome, sending the pendulum swinging back and forth. It began to count the seconds with a click. I thought once again about the heart monitor at the hospital. It nearly made me sick.

"So, this is what we're going to do, Diana," Dr. Addison began, taking her seat again. "I'm going to ask you to close your eyes and relax your body. Take deep breaths in through your nose and out through your mouth. Then, I'm going to count down from ten. When I reach the number one, you will fall into a trance-like state. It's not sleep, it's simply a high level of relaxation. Then, I'm going to lead you through the memory. I'm going to ask you questions, but you don't need to respond. You just need to let the memories come back to you. When we're done, I'll snap my fingers and you'll come back into your most conscious state of awareness. It might be a frightening experience, but just remember, you're safe with me, okay? Are you ready?"

The whole thing sounded like a load of steaming bullshit to me, but I bit my tongue and nodded, wondering what the odds were that this would actually work. Especially going into it with the level of skepticism I possessed. If anyone was stubborn enough to reject hypnosis, it was definitely me. Still, a prickle of anxiety crawled up my spine. I guess there was a part of me that was actually *hoping* it wouldn't work. I had never once wanted to remember what happened to me on Halloween night, but if it was the only way to see my attacker's face, then it was my only option. I set my jaw and closed my eyes, taking deep breaths as Dr. Addison asked me to, listening to the click of the metronome.

"Begin to relax your body," Dr. Addison said, her voice low and soothing, like the concierge at a spa. I did my best to oblige, focusing on my breath. In, out. In, out. In, out. Slowly my eyelids began to feel heavier.

"Yes, that's very good," Dr. Addison continued. "I'm going to start counting down. When I reach one you're going to wake up on the night of your assault. You're going to remember everything.

Are you ready? Ten... nine... eight...seven..."

For a moment, my instincts screamed at me to open my eyes, to run away from the memory rather than let it consume me, but my tongue felt too heavy to move and my body had gone limp. It was happening. I was slipping into an altered state of consciousness.

"Six...five...four..."

Oh god, this is a mistake. I'm not ready!

"Three... two... one."

When I opened my eyes, I was no longer in Dr. Addison's office. In fact, it seemed like I was nowhere. I spun around frantically but all I could see was dark all around me. From far away, I heard Dr. Addison's voice, like it was filtering in through water.

"You're at the party, at the game store. The Game Cave," she says, her voice echoing through the pitch-black emptiness around me. "You're in your costume. It's Halloween night."

I tried to see it, to remember what she was saying, but everything remained in the shadows.

"It's not working," I tried to scream but I couldn't form the words. I grasped at my throat uselessly.

"You're in the car now," Dr. Addison's voice said. "You're being taken to Woodley Road. It's dark outside and he's beside you. You can see his face."

Something around me shuddered. I could feel the car racing across the asphalt, bumping as it turned off the paved road and onto the dead-end dirt road. The overwhelming smell of pine-scented car air freshener and spicy deodorant mixed with sour sweat invaded my nostrils.

Still, I could see nothing around me. I couldn't see his face. My heart began to race.

"You're going into the woods now," that disembodied voice said. No, please not the woods, I thought. Suddenly an image swam into view. I gasped and recoiled but it was too late. I'm watching myself, yet looking through my own eyes as someone drags me from the car.

He's behind me, one hand over my mouth and the other wrapped around my torso and arms in a death grip. I fight with all my might but I can't break away. My feet kick wildly, sending pebbles and soil flying. For a moment, he loses his grip and I fall to the ground, screaming, doing my best to wriggle away. He's too quick though, and there's no one around to hear me, anyway.

He punches me hard in the face and I hear the cracking sound of cartilage as my nose breaks. Spots appear in my vision and warm blood spurts from my face. I start to cry as he picks me up again, dragging me further away from the road, into the woods with only the light of the moon to guide his way.

When we're deep enough behind the tree line to satisfy him, he drops me to the forest floor like a load of bricks. I try to climb to my feet, to run away, but I feel his foot collide with my ribs, knocking the wind out of me. I slump, face first in the dirt, sobbing and begging for mercy.

He flips me over. I blink away the tears and blood and mud. This is it. I'm finally going to see his face. I feel his strong arms pin my own to the ground as he swims into my vision. When the image final y takes shape I'm greeted with a sickening sight.

Staring back at me is an abhorrent beast. The Abhorrent Beast. It's not his original Halloween costume. He's changed from the deranged clown and now has become a beast, complete with a mask that obscures the true monster's face. I gulp down salty tears as he looks down at me and licks his lips.

"Who are you?" I try to scream but my mouth doesn't move. I'm helpless, trapped beneath his weight, and within the memory that I'd so long repressed. How could I have forgotten, though? It all came back so terribly easily. Somehow, I already knew what comes next.

He rips away the stocking on my face, his breathing labored. He's excited. I can feel that excitement throb against my leg. He tears my clothes open and the cold night air slices my skin.

I try to reach up and pull his mask away. If I could only get a look at his face... He smacks my hand away then hits me again. Hard. I nearly pass out and my vision goes dark again. My limbs are too heavy to move. I don't fight back anymore. It's no use. Instead, I lay perfectly still while he strips me. I don't even make a sound as he pushes himself inside of me. It hurts in a way that's unfamiliar. It takes my breath away and silent tears stream down my face while he uses my body to pleasure himself, letting out an animalistic noise as he finally finishes.

"I've been dreaming of this for a long time," he whispers hoarsely, his breath hot against my ear, "And you didn't disappoint."

His voice is familiar. I know I've heard it before. Even his smell sparks something in my memory but it slips through my fingers just as soon as I try to grasp at it. Who are you? Why can't I remember?

My tears are no longer silent. I'm sobbing now and begging for my life. In response, he backhands me, which only makes me cry more.

"Let me go," I hear my former self plead, "I won't tell anyone what happened, I promise."

"I'm afraid that's not going to happen," Dastardly Damned whispers. "This only ends one way."

I feel his hands clasp my neck. At that moment, I accept the inevitability of death. If only I could just look at him. Just one look and reliving this nightmare would be worth it.

I gasp for breath but his grasp is too tight to allow the air to pass into my lungs. My blurry vision begins to close in at the sides. It's almost over, now.

With the last ounce of my strength, I reach a single hand up and claw at his mask. I feel sweaty plastic beneath my fingertips. For a second I think I might be able to pull it off, but he turns his head away. It only slips slightly to the side, revealing a tuft of thick brown hair. I stare at it hard as I feel my life slip away. I study every strand, my only clue to the identity of my killer.

Finally, mercifully, I feel myself slip away. The last thing I hear before the consciousness is squeezed out of me is the beast whisper a final message in my ear. "You're mine now, Diana. All mine."

I woke from my trance with a gasp. Suddenly, I'm back in Dr. Addison's office with the infernal clicking of the metronome in my ears and my face slick with tears.

I shot up from the seat, half ready to fight for my life before I finally realized what was happening. Dr. Addison stared up at me wide-eyed, her hands up in the air in a position of non-threatening surrender.

"Hey, it's just me," she said, her voice still calm and soothing. "You're okay, you're in my office. The memory is far away. Just breathe."

I took a shuddering breath and collapsed back into the chair, covering my face with my hands while she continued to chant instructions.

"That's right. Just take a moment. Keep breathing. Very good."

I wiped my tears, humiliated at the show of weakness. Quickly, my panic turned to anger. I looked up at Dr. Addison, wishing that looks could kill. If they could though, she'd have been dead long ago.

"Do you want to talk about it?" Dr. Addison asked, picking up her pad and paper and resuming her normal, therapeutic posture as if she hadn't just walked me down the darkest corridor in my own mind and unlocked the most horrid memories imaginable..

I'd spent so many years convincing myself that I wasn't a victim. I'd become jaded and fearless.

I buried the dirty feeling he'd left between my legs beneath dozens of new lovers, washing his sweat away with theirs. But now, it was all as fresh as it had been when I woke from that coma nearly two years ago. The worst part, though, was that it was for nothing. I didn't even see his fucking face.

"How are you feeling? Dr. Addison tried again.

"How am I feeling?" I asked, my voice shaking with rage. "I feel sick. I feel angry. I feel victimized all over again. Is that the point of this fucked up hypnotherapy bullshit? To re-traumatize me?"

"Of course not," Dr. Addison replied. Her eyes stayed trained on me while her pen flew across the paper, documenting the specifics of my hysterics. The whole thing was too much to bear. I had to get out of there. Fast.

I stumbled to my feet and pointed at Dr. Addison with an accusatory finger.

"I can't believe you made me do that," I choked. "I had to remember it all for *nothing*. I had to relive the darkest moment of my life for *nothing*. I still don't even know who it is!"

"That's okay," Dr. Addison replied calmly. "That doesn't mean that this therapy has been a waste. I see real potential for a breakthrough. You just need to keep pushing."

"Fuck you," I spat, gathering my things and heading towards the door. "I'm never coming back here, ever again."

With that, I threw open the door and stormed out, ignoring Dr. Addison as she called out a warning after me. Let her report me to the probation board. Let her lock me up in a psych ward. I didn't care. I couldn't get lower than this.

I was finally able to catch my breath once I was seated in the driver's seat of my car with the doors locked and my head resting against the steering wheel. I tried my best to banish the awful visions from my head but they refused to go anywhere. It was all so clear, so visceral as if it happened yesterday. I could remember every detail. Every detail except for *who* had assaulted me. Unable to keep the emotions inside any longer, I slammed my first against the dashboard and screamed at the top of my lungs. It helped a little. So, I did it again. And again. And again.

I finally stopped when my voice began to crack and my throat felt raw. I took a deep breath in, cursing my hack therapist and her new-age torture techniques, and tried to figure out what to do next.

Despite everything inside me screaming not to, I cautiously walked back through the memory, gritting my teeth as the sights and smells washed over me once again. Had there been anything at all that would give me a clue as to my assailant's identity? Anything that would keep it from being a total freakin' waste? That's when it clicked. Yes. There was. His hair.

The knot in my stomach tightened as the realization washed over me. The man who kidnapped me, who beat me, raped me, choked me, and left me for dead couldn't be Caleb Mendenhall, or Henry either. I shut my eyes and remembered the weight of Dastardly Damned on top of me, flinching as I did so, trying to remember every single thing I could about his shadowy frame.

Caleb was the same height as the monster in my memory but his size was all off. His shoulders were too wide and his stomach too paunchy to match the toned, slim frame of my attacker.

Henry, on the other hand, was far too skinny. His bony arms weren't the ones that held me down in the dirt. Most damning of all, though, was that tuft of hair. Caleb had his father's thin, reddish-blonde hair, and Henry had jet black hair that nearly reached his shoulders. Neither of them possessed the thick mahogany cowlick of Dastardly Damned. I swallowed hard, trying my best to make sense of everything. A feeling of emptiness consumed me as I accepted the horrible inevitability.

Neither Caleb nor Henry had attacked me in the woods that night. It was someone else entirely. Just as much a mystery as it had been on Halloween night. I was back to square one, again.

DIRTY DIANA

Chapter 10

IT WAS A MIRACLE THAT I made it back to the group home without getting in some sort of an accident. I was so dazed I hardly saw the road ahead of me; so numb I barely noticed when an oncoming car whizzed past me, inches away, and only then realized I was drifting into the other lane. I was the shell of my former self and every bit of hope had been drained from me. I was a ghost.

When I miraculously made it to the house unharmed, I stumbled blindly through the front door and headed straight for Julian's room. I didn't knock this time, I just swung the door open and stepped inside, uninvited. It was Saturday afternoon and Julian was still in bed.

He sat up and wiped his eyes when he heard the door slam behind me. 'Diana?" he asked, his voice thick with sleep.

Wordlessly, I dropped my bag on the floor, kicked off my shoes, and crawled into his bed beside him. He stiffened with surprise. I didn't care. I just needed to be close to someone who I trusted. And Julian was somebody that fit the bill. Probably one of only two people on this planet who did.

I needed to forget. I had to fill that void within me, the one that Dastardly Damned had left when he'd torn my body and blackened my soul. After a moment, Julian relaxed a little, then a little more. Slowly his body melted into me. We lay in the twin-sized bed as our breathing synced.

"Are you okay?" he asked, his voice still scratchy and his messy hair particularly disheveled. I shook my head 'no.'

"Do you want to talk about it?" he asked, his soft eyes were sympathetic but not pitying. It made me want to cry just looking at him. Instead, I just shook my head 'no' again.

"What can I do, Diana?" he asked, nearly pleading. He brushed his fingers against my cheek, pushing away a stray strand of hair. I grabbed his hand and pressed his palm to my face.

"Kiss me again," I whispered.

Julian paused for a moment, but only a moment. Then, his lips were on mine and my hands were tangled in his hair. I kissed him with everything I had, hoping his gentle touch could wash away the stains that Dastardly Damned had left on me. I needed him now, more than anything.

More than oxygen.

I pushed him back into the pillows and climbed on top of him, lifting his shirt over his head to expose his toned stomach and olive-colored skin. He pulled my T-shirt off too; his fingers tracing my breasts; his hands moved across my body with gentle expertise. As I leaned in to kiss him again, I slowly moved my lips down across his jaw, then his neck, and finally his chest. I slowly kissed him all the way down his body, feeling goosebumps prick the flesh beneath my lips. When I reached the waistband of his pajama pants I pulled the drawstring. It was clear he wanted me, too. He was hard and I was ready. I started to pull his pants downward, and I heard him inhale sharply. Suddenly, he stopped me.

"Diana, wait," he croaked.

I felt my stomach sink. I didn't want to talk, or to think about the possible repercussions of my actions, I just wanted to intertwine my body with his and forget everything else. I didn't just want to fuck, I wanted to make love, like he said. I wanted him. The only person with whom I could take off all my clothes and still feel safe.

I looked up at his blue-grey eyes, silently begging him to forget whatever words were on his lips and just to take me, to please me, like no one else had ever been able to. Like I knew he could. I could tell by his expression that wasn't going to be the case, though. I slowly straightened up, my hands floating up toward my torso, suddenly feeling insecure.

"I can't help you hurt yourself," he whispered. "I want this. Believe me, I do, but I care about you too much to be an instrument in your self-destruction."

I leaned back; my head was spinning once again. "Is that what you think this is?" I asked. I was still sitting atop him, straddling him, and suddenly felt my cheeks flushed with embarrassment. I squirmed away, feeling ashamed that maybe Julian was right. I wasn't used to being rejected. Not because I was some prize, but simply because I only ever reached for the low hanging fruit. For a moment, I felt like the old Diana; the awkward, unpopular virgin who no one would look at twice. Except for a predator.

"I don't know, is it?" Julian asked. "Or is this..."

I knew what he was asking, but I didn't have an answer. How could I when my whole world was crashing down around me? I pushed myself off of him and shuffled to the end of the bed feeling angry and humiliated and utterly alone, my hands wrapping around my nude body as if to hide my nakedness from him.

Just when I thought things couldn't possibly get worse, I heard a knock at the door.

"Shit," Julian mumbled, his hands fumbling among the twisted sheets of his bed to find his sweatshirt.

"Fuck," I exclaimed at the same time, reaching for my shoes.

It was too late though. As soon as Edna heard voices through the door, she swung it open, her eyes landing on two guilty-looking faces. The worst part was, she didn't even look surprised, just disappointed. Disappointed and tired. I had to give it to her; the timing was truly impeccable.

I pulled my shirt over my head and cleared my throat to make an excuse but Edna just shook her head.

"I warned you, both of you," she said, "And now I've reached the end of my rope. Julian, I'm going to have to write up a citation for you. It's going in your file and to the probation board. And as for you, Diana? I'm very sorry, but you're going to have to leave immediately."

"Leave?" I asked incredulously. Julian and I exchanged panicked looks. "Where am I supposed to go?"

"That will be up to the probation officers assigned to your case, and the court," Edna replied sternly. "I'm going to go make a call now. I need you both to get dressed and Diana, I need you to pack your things. I'm sorry to do this, but it's the only way. I can't have you compromising the integrity of this operation with your antics. Be ready when the officers arrive."

Without another word, Edna turned on her heel and stomped down the hall to her office, leaving me and Julian thunderstruck in her wake.

My mind immediately began to race again. Was this for real? Was I going to *jail*? I stumbled to my feet and looked back at Julian, who was pulling on his sweatshirt, the look of panic on his face answered that question.

"We can fix this," he said, almost pleadingly.

"You've done enough," I replied. My monotone voice sounded like a soulless robot and internally, I felt just as lifeless. It was wrong for me to blame him for something I had clearly initiated. "I'm sorry," I murmured. I had to get out of there before the police showed up. It was too much to even think about, being thrown in the back of a cruiser and shuffled into some dank, dark jail cell. I couldn't let that happen.

"Wait, Diana, please..." Julian said, getting to his feet. I jerked away, unable to look at his handsome face. I didn't want to put him at any further risk by dragging him into my own drama. My own destruction. He was right. I was hell bent on self-destruction. I wouldn't take him with me. Without so much as another glance back, I rushed to my room next door and began throwing things into a backpack. Mismatched socks, a stained pair of jeans, anything that was within arms reach. Through the paper-thin walls of the house, I could hear the garbled voice of Edna on the phone. By the time she'd hung up the call, though, I was already on my way out the door.

I threw my backpack into the passenger seat and jammed the key into the ignition. I didn't know where I was going, I just knew I had to get away. Fast. Edna watched me from the window, her arms crossed and her head swiveling back and forth. She didn't try to stop me, though. She knew better. The car's engine stalled once and then blessedly purred to life.

Seconds later I was speeding down the road, my nails biting into the steering wheel from the force of my grip.

I flew along the road, turning randomly, putting as much distance between myself and the halfway house as I could. When I finally felt like I had gone far enough, I pulled off to the shoulder of the road and caught my breath. My hands fumbled through my bag, searching for my phone. I grabbed it and shakily punched in a number that I'd committed to memory. There was only one person I could call when everyone else had turned their back on me. It rang twice.

Then, a familiar voice answered.

"Hey kiddo," Alex said, his chipper greeting a stark contrast to the devastating situation I'd found myself in. I cleared my throat. I didn't want him to know I was crying. I never cried. Not anymore.

"Hi," I breathed, "I'm really sorry to call you like this. I just didn't know what else to do. I need your help..."

"Anything," Alex responded immediately. "What's going on, Diana? Tell me what you need."

For the first time all day, I felt some semblance of being okay.

DIRTY DIANA

Chapter 11

MINE AND ALEX'S RELATIONSHIP had never been the same after my attack. At first, he'd been protective over me. Too protective, even. He wanted to keep me in his sight at all times. He hovered over me at all hours of the day, walking me from class to class and staring at me as I sat at the kitchen table and struggled through my homework. I suppose he must have felt guilty.

After all, he was the one who was supposed to pick me up from Game Cave that night. He claimed that he'd only been ten minutes late because his car keys had been moved from their usual place, but when he arrived I was already gone. I'm not sure if he ever forgave himself and to be honest, I hadn't done my part to let him off the hook. Nothing that happened was his fault, but if I couldn't remember the details, it was easier for me to simply create a distance between us. And that distance, over time, had stretched longer and wider. I'd never even been to his apartment before. A person can only be pushed away so many times before they stop fighting for you. Still, no matter what, I knew my big brother would be there for me when shit hit the fan, and he hadn't disappointed.

By the time I reached the apartment complex, on the outskirts of town near the college campus, the sun had nearly sunk below the horizon. The boxy, unassuming building was backlit by a dazzling sunset. Not that I was in any state to appreciate it. I parked my car in an empty space and double-checked the address he'd sent me. Then, I climbed out of my car and ascended the outside staircase to the second floor and knocked on Apartment 2F.

I hadn't told Alex everything. I might, eventually, but when I called him from the side of the road, I didn't have the time nor the stamina to explain the strange sequence of events that led me to his door. I only said that I'd been kicked out of the group home, halfway house, whatever you wanted to call it, due to a misunderstanding. It would be cleared up in no time, I promised him, but until then I needed somewhere to stay. He'd agreed without hesitation, though I wasn't sure how much of my story he believed.

When he opened the door, I was greeted by a carefree smile that immediately put me at ease.

"I thought you might have gotten lost," he joked, wrapping me up in a half-hug. I forced a small laugh and hugged him back. "Come in," he said, taking my bag and shutting the door behind me. "Make yourself comfortable. Cool hair."

"Thanks," I said, returning his smile. "I like yours as well." It was a lame attempt at a joke because Alex was the type of guy who always kept his hair neat and trimmed, no added color. He was so blessed with handsomeness that doing anything different would tamper with perfection.

There wasn't much to the small apartment. A tiny kitchen and living area decorated with posters of sports teams I didn't recognize or care about, a big TV that commanded the largest wall, and three doors, one for both bedrooms and the bathroom, lined the other. I sat down on the sofa and forced myself to relax as I took in the scene. Alex dropped my bag in a recliner and put his hands on his hips, smiling down at me expectantly.

"Nice spot," I said half-heartedly.

"It gets the job done," Alex replied. "I'm glad you're here. Even under the circumstances... Well, it's always nice to see you. It's been a while, Sis."

"You too, Alex," I replied earnestly. I already felt the more like a normal human than I had all day, though that wasn't saying much.

"I'm sure you remember this guy," he said, as one of the bedroom doors swung open and a figure appeared. I turned my head and caught sight of a familiar face. One I hadn't seen in God knows how long.

He'd buzzed his head and grown his beard out but his charming smile was unmistakable.

"Hey, Brian," I said excitedly, flashing a smile his way. "Are you guys roomies?" I asked.

"We are," Alex replied.

Brian was obviously taken by surprise. He was dressed in nothing but a towel, wrapped around his waist, and water from a recent shower dripped down his back and chest. His mouth made a perfect circle when he saw me sitting on his couch, then his face broke into a devilish smile.

"Well hey there," he piped up. "Sorry I didn't dress for the occasion, Diana. I wasn't expecting to see you."

"Yeah, sorry man," Alex said, "It was a last minute thing. I hope you don't mind if she spends the night on the couch tonight."

"Of course not," Brian replied, flashing me a wink. He crossed to the fridge and pulled out a bottle of beer, then opened it with his teeth.

"I'd come give you a hug, but..." he said, gesturing to his half-naked body, "your brother would probably castrate me," he finished with a chuckle. Then, he reached back into the fridge and grabbed another beer, extending it toward me. "Want one?"

"Dude, she's barely nineteen," Alex interjected, looking at me wearily.

"Chill Alex. Do you remember what we were getting into when we were nineteen?" Brian replied cheekily. "Give the girl a break. It's just one beer and she looks like she could use it."

Brian was right about that. Alex shrugged and Brian opened the beer for me.

"Just one," Alex said, unable to hold back his protective nature.

Brian and I clinked the necks of the bottles together and I took a long drink, enjoying the rush of tranquility it brought me. I sighed and reclined back into the couch, closing my eyes. I heard Brian snicker.

"See?"

I had more than one beer that night. In fact, I had more than I could count. After the chaos of the past few days, it felt so good to shut the world away and get drunk with two people who knew nothing about my current predicament. I quickly glossed over the reason for my expulsion and sudden arrival at their doorstep, quickly changing the subject to whatever sports game played on TV, feigning interest. Apparently, Alex and Brian had kept up the ritual of watching all things sports on weekends. Liz was going to school on the west coast so it kept Alex out of trouble. As far as Brian, I wasn't sure what his romance status was these days.

We sat on the couch for a couple of hours, watching the testosterone-filled men collide into one another over and over. Brian snuck fresh beers over to me every time Alex left the room to pee, always shooting me one of his signature, sly winks. Before, when he'd do that, or complement the way I looked, I'd blush and trip over my words. A lot had changed since then, though, and now I matched his flirtatious banter, much to my brother's discomfort. I was too buzzed to care though, riding the temporary high. I sat between the two on the couch, cracking jokes, forgetting about the world outside, enjoying the beer buzz and the safety of the four walls that surrounded me.

By the time midnight rolled around, we were all giggly and buzzed and I was completely exhausted.

Alex stretched and yawned, checking the time pointedly. "I think it's time to call it a night," he said, ruffling my hair like a kid. Normally, I might have minded, but the beers had taken away my bite. "Let me grab you a blanket and some pillows," he offered.

Alex got up and disappeared into his room. Immediately I felt Brian's eyes on me. I smirked, knowing that he was staring. Suddenly, I was overtaken by that hollow ache. I looked over at him from the corner of my eye and batted my lashes.

"You look really great, Diana," he purred, his voice low enough that Alex wouldn't hear. "You've grown into a real beauty."

"Are you *flirting* with your best friend's little sister, Brian?" I asked, my tongue thick between my lips. I giggled involuntarily.

"Only if she wants me to be flirting with her," he replied.

I could hear Alex's footsteps approaching from the bedroom. Just before he emerged with a quilt and pillow I mouthed the words '*I do.*'

"Thanks, Alex," I said, turning my gaze away from Brian. He got up from the couch and cracked his neck, then slowly meandered toward his bedroom, floating in the doorway as Alex and I set up the makeshift bed. When everything was in place, Alex mussed my hair again and gave me a soft smile.

"'Night, Diana," he said. "I'm going to give Liz a call and then crash for the night."

"'Night, Alex. Tell Liz I said 'hey.'"

"'Night, guys," Brian added. Alex rolled his eyes and chuckled, then made his way back into his bedroom, snapping off the lights and shutting the door behind him. The room was suddenly still and awfully quiet.

I sat back down on the couch but Brian remained unmoved, leaning in the doorway, his eyes scanning me up and down. I felt the need increase; the need to be touched and seen and fucked. The fact that it was wrong only made me want to do it more. I bit my lip and glanced back at Alex's door. Brian smiled. Maybe I'd feel guilty about it tomorrow. But then again, maybe not.

"You might be more comfortable sleeping in my bed," Brian said, his husky voice so quiet it was almost inaudible. I only thought about it briefly. My body reacted before my brain. Julian's rejection earlier still gnawed at my self-esteem. Brian stood aside and pushed open his bedroom door and I, treading as lightly as I could, padded across the hardwood floors and entered the shadowy abode.

He closed the door and the darkness nearly swallowed us whole. I stumbled, drunk and dizzy, through the pitch black with my arms outstretched, fumbling around until I made contact with something soft. Yep, that was a bed, my drunk brain clearly said.

"Oops," I exclaimed, chuckling doltishly as I tumbled into the sheets.

"Shh!" Brian commanded and I clapped my hand over my mouth to shut myself up.

"Sorry, I'm tipsy," I whispered. Brian didn't reply. My eyes began to adjust to the dark. From my position sprawled across the bed, I looked up at the shadowy outline of Brian, standing over the bed. I blinked until my vision wasn't doubled then extended a hand out to him.

"Are you just gonna stand there all night or are you gonna join me?" I asked, trying my best to sound less drunk and more sexy. What was he waiting for? Isn't this what he wanted?

Brian was still and silent for another beat. Then, in a single swift movement, he was on top of me. The sudden weight of his body left me breathless.

He kissed me hard. He pushed his mouth so forcefully against me that I could feel his teeth behind his lips. After a moment of surprise, I kissed him back, trying to find a comfortable place to rest my hands. My head started to spin so I made a move to pull away to catch my breath. Brian only kissed me more aggressively, shoving his tongue into my mouth and grabbing my head tight with his hands. The taste of stale beer overtook my senses. There was something about the way he touched me that made me feel suddenly sick. It was beyond passion, more like hostility, but more than that it also felt strangely... familiar.

Finally, I was able to turn my head to the side long enough to catch my breath. I took a deep inhale through my nose as Brian pressed himself into me. His rigid cock throbbed against my thigh boldly. I could smell the sour, salty stench of his sweat mixed with spicy deodorant. All of a sudden my stomach dropped.

I *knew* that smell. That cologne and that lingering stench he didn't seem to be able to wash off. I recognized the feeling of his body on top of me. There was a reason it was all so familiar. Before that afternoon, I wouldn't have known. Back then, I didn't remember, but I did now. The paralyzing sensation of pure dread overtook me. Before I could open my mouth to scream, I felt something collide with my head, hard. Then, there was nothing at all.

DIRTY DIANA

Chapter 12

WHEN I CAME TO I WAS in the backseat of Brian's car. It was like waking up in a nightmare. It was the worst possible case of déjà vu. The first thing I noticed was the rumble of the car across the asphalt, just like when I was under hypnosis. Next, I was struck by the smell of a pine-scented car freshener. I didn't want to open my eyes. I knew all too well what I would see. I couldn't help myself, though. I'd never been a master of self-control.

My head screamed as soon as the streetlight hit my eyes. I could feel a throbbing lump on my temple and my face was sticky with blood. My arms and legs had been duct-taped together and two more pieces made an 'X' over my mouth. Against my will, a soft moan escaped.

Brian turned around and smiled.

"Good morning, sleepyhead," he cooed. Anger and disgust pricked at me as he spoke. I wanted to vomit, but with my mouth taped shut, there was nowhere for it to go. Instead, I bit the inside of my lip until I tasted blood.

"I was worried you might not wake up for a minute there," Brian continued, speaking as casually as he had when he was discussing the football games we'd all watched yesterday. For some reason, his calm demeanor was even more terrifying than raving madness. He was smiling. It was evil. Like the smile of The Joker. I felt a shiver electrify my body.

"I got you pretty good. It was the bedside lamp, in case you're curious. Not the most optimal choice, but I had to make do."

I felt the car swerve and Brian turned his eyes back on the road. As we flew through the dark night, memories came rushing back. I closed my eyes and let them invade my psyche. These were memories that hadn't surfaced during my hypnotherapy session with Dr. Addison. Horrific memories that were buried so deep in the recesses of my subconscious mind that nothing but a replay of that traumatic event with the same players could cut them loose. I'd wanted answers after all and now those answers were playing out like a horror flick I was both watching and reliving at the same time. I couldn't stop the confettied pieces of that night as they replayed now.

It's the night of Halloween. I'm standing outside the Game Cave waiting for Alex to pick me up.

I'm sad and embarrassed. I was stood up by Dastardly Damned. After all the hours we'd spent chatting and playing games, he'd bailed on me without so much as a text. Typical. It was just my luck. I was doomed to be friendless and celibate for life, it seemed. I check my watch. Alex is late.

I see headlights turning into the lot. I look around and see that no one else is waiting. It must be Alex. As the car comes closer, though, I see a different face smiling at me from the driver's seat.

Brian pulls up in front of me and rolls down the window. "Hey, your brother passed out so I figured that I'd come and pick you up. Hop in!" He calls, waving me toward the passenger side door.

I pause. It seems unlike Alex to leave me stranded, especially when he knows how much trouble he'll be in with our mom. I look around the empty lot for a moment, then back at Brian, who's still smiling.

"C'mon, you want to walk home or something?" he asks playfully, gesturing me toward him again. I make a mental note to hold this over Alex's head the next time I get the chance or need a little leverage, then climb inside the car with Brian. Thank goodness someone is looking out for me. I snap my seatbelt into place and Brian locks the doors before we zoom away.

"By now I guess you've figured it out," Brian said, chuckling to himself, "It's too little too late, though. This time I plan to finish what I started nearly three years ago."

He looked back at me, a wicked smile on his face, but his eyes were as dead and cold as could be. He looked like a rotting Jack-'O-Lantern, two weeks after Halloween.

"It's kind of nice, isn't it?" he asked, hardly able to contain his excitement, "To have D-10 and Dastardly Damned back together again? I've been waiting for this reunion a long, long time."

We pass by the exit to my house. I open my mouth to say something, but before I can even get a word out, Brian's already talking.

"I'm taking a shortcut," he grins, "Just trust me."

I shrug and sink down in my seat.

"So, how did it go with your internet boyfriend?" Brian asks. He's looking at me without blinking as the car slowly drifts into the next lane. His pupils are dilated and his eyes are glassy. I clear my throat and look out the windshield pointedly but Brian doesn't seem to notice. It isn't until another car honks at him that he straightens out the wheel and momentarily looks away. He's high on something I can tell.

He's acting strange.

"The internet guy? He bailed on me," I reply, my cheeks burning with embarrassment. Brian gives me a look I can't describe. It makes me feel itchy.

"I'm sorry Diana, that's a bummer. Do you really like this guy?"

I shrug and look out the window, feeling uneasy about his interest in my personal life.

"C'mon you can tell me the truth," Brian adds.

"Um, I guess I do. Or at least, I did," I mumble.

"Were you attracted to him?" Brian asks. My eyes dart towards him, but I'm too bashful to maintain contact. His questions feel a little off but still, I say nothing.

"I don't really know," I say. "I've never even met him."

"What if you have?" he asks.

I chuckle nervously to myself. That'd be a trip, I thought to myself.

"Did you want him to fuck you?" Brian asks. I feel my stomach go sour.

"You're being weird, Brian," I tell him half-heartedly. He laughs in a way that I've never heard him laugh before. It's high-pitched and giddy. For some reason it makes me feel even more unsettled.

"So, did you?"

I swallow hard and shrug again.

"I don't know, maybe, but it doesn't matter anyway. He didn't show up. That's that."

The car is silent for a moment. I glance at the speedometer and am shocked to see we're going over eighty miles per hour. I look around and see nothing familiar. This is no shortcut. We have to be lost. I want to say something but Brian interjects again.

"Diana," Brian finally says, pressing on the accelerator even more, until the dark trees and thinning houses become a blur, "What if I told you that Dastardly Damned did show up? What if I told you he's been looking forward to this night for a long time? What about if I told you that you're in the car with him right now?"

Brian was silent for the rest of the drive. In the backseat, I fought with everything in me to loosen my restraints without catching his attention. There was only one thought in my mind, one driving force keeping me from losing my mind entirely. Survive.

Brian pulled onto a dirt road, the car wobbling as it transitioned from the smooth pavement to the pothole puckered side street. He was taking me back to the place where it happened. The place where he tried to kill me. It's clear what his intention is. He wants me dead, once and for all.

I'd managed to loosen the tape slightly. Not enough to slip out but I was close. I only needed a moment more but Brian wasted no time. He pulled off into a shallow ditch and turned off the car, thrusting everything around us into complete darkness. Then he took a deep, satisfied breath and let out a languid sigh.

"You have no idea how long you've occupied my mind, Diana," he said, his eyes far away, directed above at the stars that dotted the clear night sky. "I watched you grow up, you know? Sure, I was a kid too, but I've known you for what feels like forever. Now, after all these years, I'm finally going to possess you. By the end of the night, you'll belong to me; mind, body, and soul."

A barrage of filthy insults piled up behind my taped-shut lips. He was lucky that I hadn't broken free. Because if I had, I would gouge his eyes out with my bare hands. With no mask to hide behind this time, it would be all that much easier.

"I guess I never gave you much of an explanation, last time," he continued. "Not that it matters much anyway. My secrets will die with you very soon. But maybe that's why I feel safe to divulge them."

He turned around and grinned at me again.

"There's not really even a reason, anyway. None except that I wanted you to be mine. Of course, your brother would never have allowed that. Even if I tried to do things the right way. The right way probably wouldn't have been enough to satiate my needs, anyway. I've always had some very... specific proclivities. It's just not as fun to fuck when a woman wants it, you know? I'd like to blame the acid I'd done that night, but that only made it more palpable."

"Wait, Brian, are you joking with me right now? You're Dastardly Damned?" I ask in a quaking voice.

"Surprise," he replies. I feel like I'm going to faint.

"But how? Why?" I stutter.

"What do you mean?" he asks as if the whole thing should make perfect sense. "Don't you think that the effort I put in was romantic? Don't you see the lengths I went to for your attention? I thought for sure once you knew that you'd be excited, We're finally meeting for the first time, Diana. Truly."

When I look at Brian again his smile has suddenly fallen. The light from the dashboard makes his eyes look hollow. I realize that I'm frightened of him.

"Please just take me home?" I ask, my voice breaking pitifully. Brian's unhappy face contorts in rage.

"I thought you liked Dastardly Damned. You have so much in common, after all. You said yourself you were attracted to him... To me."

"Please, Brian, just take me-"

Suddenly a fist flies at me from the driver's seat. It collides with my jaw and I hear something pop. I yell out in pain and start to cry. The ferocity of the blow is animalistic. I suddenly realize how far away from home I am and how empty the long, dark stretch of road really is.

"You see what you made me do, Diana?" Brian asks, his breathing labored. I look out the window, praying to see a familiar landmark or a cop car, but there's nothing but trees. I try to pull open the door, but Brian yanks my wrist away and puts me in a headlock. I beat against his arms to no avail. He's able to hold me down and drive simultaneously with ease. I'm no match for him.

But why does he want to hurt me in the first place? None of this makes sense. I blackout again. When I come to, he's wearing the Zombie Clown costume. He's smoking something, and I cough and wheeze as he approaches. "Care for a hit? Best crack in town," he says, holding the pipe out and laughing maniacally. His foot kicks my face, and everything goes blessedly dark.

The next thing I see is that I'm lying on the ground with the moon illuminating the sky, allowing me to see nothing but trees that are now leave-less and the deafening sound of silence. Finally,

I hear the sound of dead leaves crunching under the weight of someone's approaching footsteps coming closer to where I lie. My eyes have adjusted to the darkness and that's when, to my horror, I see that Brian is now wearing the costume I recognize as The Abhorrent Beast.

I quickly realized that I now had the whole detailed picture of what transpired that night more than two years ago. The horror which led up to the memories unlocked during my hypnotherapy session. My mind had buried the identity of the monster all this time because it was simply too horrific to recall. But, at the moment, it served to clue me in as what to expect as Brian administered his brutality in a twisted replay of that night. He was crazed and insane. His eyes were dead.

I hurled insults at the dastardly bastard despite the tape on my mouth. I wanted to hurt him, to put my hands on him, but I'd have wanted to hear my screams of rage as I did so. I recoiled as he reached toward me, but he grabbed the back of my neck with one hand and ripped the tape off my mouth with his other, leaving a stinging, sticky mess behind. The first thing I did was spit. A glob of saliva landed on his cheek and I savored the single, solitary second of satisfaction as his eyes went white with rage. In an instant, he collected himself and wiped it away, shaking his head back and forth like a disappointed parent.

"You've really toughened up since our last encounter. I suppose you can thank me for that. You were a girl back then. A victim. But I made you a woman and, accidentally, a survivor. It was a mistake, sure, but everything happens for a reason. It will make it all the more satisfying this time. I like it when girls fight back."

"You're twisted and insane," I spat. "Demented. Sick in the fucking head. I'm not scared of you though. You know why? Because only a coward and a *pussy* beats up on little girls. That's what you are. A scared little boy who never got the balls to pick on someone his own size. A pathetic eunuch!"

I could tell I was beginning to get to him. His jaw tightened and he slapped me across the cheek. It stung like hell, but I hardly noticed it. Good, I thought, get angry. Get sloppy. Make a mistake. It was my only hope of survival.

"Did you ever see me, peeking through the crack in your bedroom door, watching you sleep in that big pink four-poster bed? God, I loved watching you sleep. Knowing that your family was there too, just feet away, that I could be caught at any moment? I mean that was a thrill."

"If I saw you I would have screamed. I would have told Alex there was a monster watching me. You would have never stepped foot in our house again."

"Well, then it's a good thing that never happened," Brian chuckled. "I think that's enough out of you for now, though," he added, reaching out to replace the tape across my face. I jerked away, trying my best not to let the frightened whimper in my throat escape.

"Just answer one thing," I said breathlessly, just before I was rendered silent again. Brian paused and raised an eyebrow. They were dark and thick, like his hair used to be before he buzzed it all off. No wonder I hadn't put it together. It was all a part of his twisted plan.

"Why me?" I hissed. A smile played across his lips.

"Because you're different, Diana. You're not like every other girl in this town. You were unique and sweet and ripe for the taking. So, I took you. Does that make sense?"

"Yeah, perfect sense," I spat. "Sounds like you couldn't get any fucking ass."

His smile fell and he slapped the tape back over my mouth...hard. He was done with my games now, I could tell. He was fuming and the tension was building. I was treading a dangerous line, but what other choice did I have? As he got out of the car, opened the back door, and slung me over his shoulder the same thought repeated over and over again, even louder than before.

Survive.

He didn't notice when I slipped the tape off my wrists. If he had, it certainly would have been the end, but he was too busy muttering under his breath what he planned to do to me. I didn't listen.

I couldn't. If I did, I might lose my nerve. Instead, I put every iota of my concentration at the task at hand, and soon my hands were free. Sweat pricked my palms. I held my hands together as if they were still restrained, keeping up appearances until the moment was right to strike. I needed the element of surprise on my side.

After what felt like a lifetime, Brian finally slowed his pace. I knew where we were without even looking up. It was the clearing I'd visited under hypnosis only hours earlier. Suddenly, I felt Brian release his grip on me and I tumbled to the ground, hitting the dirt carpet of the forest with a thud.

He rolled me onto my back and looked down at me, his face a mask of horror. It took every ounce of self-control not to try and run as he began to run his hands down my body, grasping at my soft flesh hard enough to leave bruises. He slowly crawled on top of me and for the second time that night, I could feel the throbbing proof of his excitement pressed against me. Everything about the scene was all too familiar.

"I should warn you, this isn't going to be as good for you as it is for me," he whispered hoarsely in my ear. He pushed my arms above my head then I felt his fingertips clamor down toward the zipper of my jeans. This was it. I had to make my move before it was too late. If I died trying... well, at least I'd deny him the pleasure of a warm body. But as sick and twisted as he was, I wouldn't put necrophilia past him at all.

I waited just a few more horrifying seconds as Brian pulled down his pants. I didn't want to but I knew it might save me even just a few moments when I made a break for it, and those few moments could be the difference between life and death. I nearly retched as I felt his warm flesh against mine. It was time.

Everything happened in a flash. My hands, which were outstretched above my head, suddenly sprang into action, grasping at anything around them I might be able to use as a weapon. By the time Brian realized I'd broken free of my restraints, it would be too late. My right hand closed around something hard. A rock, the size of a baseball. Without hesitation, I swung the rock hard at the side of his head. It collided with a satisfying crack that reverberated between the trees.

Brian cried out in pain and rolled off me, clutching his wound. I took the opportunity to bring the rock down again, this time aiming it at the duct tape wrapped around my feet. The impact had the intended effect. The already loose tape ripped just enough to allow me to jerk my legs apart. Then, before Brian could even stumble to his feet, I was bolting through the trees in the dead of night, screaming at the top of my lungs.

DIRTY DIANA

Chapter 13

HIS FOOTSTEPS POUNDED against the ground behind me. He was close but I didn't dare turn around. I zigzagged through the trees, stumbling over roots and bushes, my clothes snagging on limbs which also sliced my face like razor blades. My lungs burned with exertion but I willed myself to push on. I was so close to escaping. To freedom. To Safety.

Suddenly, I felt a buzz in my back pocket. My heart went into my throat. Brian had made a critical mistake. Though last time, he'd taken my cell phone, this time I'd surprised him before he had the chance. Without slowing my pace, I ripped the phone from my pocket and fumbled to answer the call.. I didn't care who was on the other line. I just needed someone to hear me.

I finally managed to slide it open but I was breathless. I couldn't form words. Brian's labored breathing and heavy footfall was still close at my heels.

"Hey, Diana, it's me," a familiar voice said, crackling through the receiver. I nearly wept with relief. It was Julian. "Listen, I just want to apologize for earlier-" he started, stopping short when he finally heard my panting. I choked and tried to catch my breath just enough to form the words. It felt like a hundred daggers were piercing my lungs.

"What's wrong?" Julian asked quickly. Where to even start...

"He's got me…" I croaked, gasping for air between words. "Dastardly Damned… He brought me to the place… where he tried to kill me… The woods… Please help…. Call the police."

Julian started to reply but a sharp double beep from my phone told me the call had dropped. I couldn't be sure if he even heard or understood me. I felt my heart sink.

"I'm going to get you, Diana," Brian called. His breathing didn't sound as ragged as my own.

This was a race of stamina and I was set to lose. He couldn't be more than thirty or forty feet behind me, his tennis shoes crunching over the dead leaves that littered the forest floor. It was nearly Halloween, I suddenly realized. Almost three full years since we'd been here, like this, before.

A new cramp between my bottom ribs suddenly made me double over and nearly fall to the ground. I gasped in pain. It was time to make a snap decision. With the last of my strength, I launched myself behind an old oak tree. I covered my mouth to muffle the whimpers and pants that threatened to slip. I had to be quiet. Quiet enough for Brian to walk right by. Though my lungs begged for fresh oxygen, I held my breath.

Seconds later, I heard his rapid footsteps pass right by me. He paused, only for a fraction of a moment just a few feet past where I had been standing. I stayed frozen, still as a statue, fighting every natural urge in my body. Then, I heard my monster huff with anger and frustration before he took off running in the wrong direction.

"I'll find you, you little bitch! I'll make you pay," he yelled, but his voice was growing farther and farther away. I could have cried from relief if I'd had the time, but I wasn't in the clear yet. I got unsteadily to my feet and looked around, trying to decide what direction to go. From my left, I heard the mechanical hum of an engine in the distance. Jackpot. With one last deep breath, I gathered the rest of my strength and began to run full force toward the sound.

I don't know how far or for how long I ran. The wooded area couldn't be too big, but somehow the trees seemed infinite. What I do know, however, is that when I finally stumbled into the street I was nearly plowed right down by an oncoming car.

I raised my arms defensively as if that would have made a difference, and the car screeched to a halt only inches away from me. The smell of burnt rubber filled the air. I slammed my fist down on the hood of the car and started to scream. I don't know if I was actually forming words, or just shrieking like a banshee. Either way, it had the desired effect. The driver climbed out of the car and approached me. I reached out to whomever it was, begging for help, and as the form took shape I felt a wave of relief wash over me.

The man rushed to me as I slumped against the hunter-green Volvo. A familiar pair of arms wrapped around me. Somehow, someway, Julian had found me.

I collapsed into uncontrollable sobs. Julian stroked my hair and helped me to the car, wiping viscous blood away from my tear-streaked face. He whispered comforting words into my ear but I didn't hear him. Nothing felt real. It wasn't until I was seated in the passenger seat of his car with the doors locked that I finally allowed myself to believe that I had survived.

"The ambulance is on its way, okay?" Julian said, holding my hand so tight it nearly lost feeling.

"H-how did you get here so fast?" I asked, my voice no more than a broken whisper.

"I was night-fishing at the reservoir. I do that to clear my head sometimes. I remembered you once told me about the Woodley Road area where you'd been assaulted. After our call was dropped and you mentioned Dastardly Damned, well I put two and two together. It's a miracle I was so close. I even beat the cops here."

I nodded, trying my best to catch my breath, trying to make sense of the nightmare that surrounded me. It was all going to be okay, though, I reminded myself. I made it. I survived Dastardly Damned once again.

"Who the fuck did this to you?" Julian asked, his voice filled with vitriol. I'd never heard his voice as harsh and angry as it was right now. I opened my mouth to respond but just as I did, a figure stumbled into the road in front of us, caught in the car's beams like a deer in headlights. He shielded his eyes from the sudden brightness, wincing as his hand bumped against a bloody wound on his head.

There was no need for me to answer Julian's question, now. He took one look at Brian, standing wild-eyed and blood-spattered in the middle of the street, and he knew.

"That's him, isn't it?" Julian asked. His voice was flat and calm. Eerily calm. I nodded, unable to take my eyes off Brian as he struggled to catch a glimpse of us through the foggy windshield.

Julian looked back at him too and nodded again, matter-of-factly. Before either of us could say a word, he pushed the gear shift from park into drive and suddenly we were barreling, at top speed, toward Dastardly Damned.

Brian realized a moment too late what was happening. He didn't even have time to turn around. That meant I got to enjoy the expression on his face as Julian rammed the car straight into him.

I swear, when I think back to that moment, I relive it in slow motion. The vehicle hit his body with a thud, splattering blood across the hood. Then we felt the wheels go over a bump and there was a wet, popping noise from beneath the car that I can recall perfectly to this day.

Once the back wheels had cleared Brian's limp body, Julian hit the brakes. We waited, for a moment, half expecting him to get up. No such luck for Brian, though. I watched from the rearview mirror as a pool of blood began to spread across the pavement, glistening like rubies in the light.

I looked at Julian, my body tingling all over. His expression was still strangely calm. I reached my hand out and touched his face. Then, he turned to me, smiling weakly, and put his hand atop mine, nuzzling closer to it.

"Now you don't have to hurt yourself anymore," he whispered. "Finally, the right person got hurt. You're free."

Tears flowed fast down my face. I was stunned, grateful, terrified, relieved, and panicky all at once. I tried to form words but Julian shook his head and gently placed his finger to my lips. In the distance, we could hear the sound of sirens approaching.

"Diana, listen to me," Julian said, grabbing me by both shoulders and looking deep into my weeping eyes. "Everything is going to be alright. You don't need to cover for me. Just tell the truth. I'll be fine."

I processed the words for a moment then shook my head no. "He ran out into the road," I said slowly, my voice barely audible. "You hit him by accident. That's all there was to it. Nobody is to blame but his crazy ass."

Despite everything, I finally felt myself smile. Relief washed over me like a hot bath. The sirens were closer now. They were so close we could see the lights. I almost felt the urge to giggle. He was dead. My demon was dead.

"Thank you," I whispered to Julian. Now it was his turn to smile, too. We sat there like that for a minute, a survivor and a murderer, grinning at each other like madmen. Then, I wrapped my arms around Julian and squeezed with all my might. He met my embrace, burying his head in my filthy, purple hair.

"He's gone, Diana," he whispered. "He's really gone."

I had lost consciousness by the time first responders arrived. Julian said I still had a smile on my face, even as they put me on a stretcher and loaded me into the ambulance.

Unfortunately for Julian, though, he was left to answer a lot of tough questions. Brian, on the other hand, had no one left to answer to but God. He was proclaimed dead upon impact. An understandable accident, given the nature of that evening's events.

Who could have foreseen him running out onto Woodley Road like that?

It took a long time for Alex to come to grips with everything. Brian had been his best friend, after all, but when he stood beside me at the press conference when they announced my attacker had perished in a life or death struggle, Alex didn't shed a tear. Like all of us, he made his way to the other side somehow. Between the two of us, Dr. Addison would be able to buy a yacht.

And as for me? Well, I won't lie. It took a while to process the whole thing. When I woke up in the hospital the next morning, it would have been easier to believe that it was all a dream. I'd suffered from shock and dehydration.

In time, though, I was relieved to find that I *was* actually doing better. It didn't happen immediately. There was no dramatic or magical moment of revelation. I just slowly felt the empty, dark void inside of me close up. And one day when I looked in the mirror, the face I saw reflected back at me was totally unfamiliar, yet welcomed. I was no longer, *Dirty Diana*, a victim, or a survivor. I was just Diana again. And everything really was alright.

I was allowed to move back into the group home and serve the rest of my probation without further penalty. In retrospect, I was pretty lucky that so many people in the system were sympathetic to my situation, and impressed that I had finally taken a sincere and active role in my recovery.

I even graduated high school, barely, thanks to Julian's help. After that night, our friendship became unbreakable. We shared a secret and it bound us together for life. Luckily, we didn't mind being wrapped up together. That friendship did, eventually, blossom into love. Julian never cut himself again.

Years came and went and I stopped dreading Halloween. I'd gone up against my own personal nightmare and bested him, after all. There was nothing in the world that could scare me now. I was a new person, born from the ashes of my former self, and it felt great. Life went on and so did I.

Throughout it all though, no matter how much time passed, one thing remained unchanged. I never made any new friends on the internet, ever again.

Julian and I have carved out a life together. He finished college and works as the administer at the local Head Start Program. I, on the other hand, work as a receptionist at Project Woman, a shelter here in town that houses battered women and their children while they await legal disposition of the criminal charges pending on their respective abusers. It's a safe house in layman's terms, and if I said nothing could shock me any longer, I'd be lying.

I wish a happy and safe future for all of those who have or will suffer at the hands of an abuser or worse.

Peace Out.

The End

Sneak Peek

DO YOU ENJOY TWISTED New Adult Suspense like "Dirty Diana?" If so, how about a sneak peek of "Southern Comfort," inspired by actual events?

Here's the background for why I wrote this book:

Please note: This book is loosely based on true events which occurred in a small Southern town in the mid-1950's. A diary was found in the attic of a house that a relative of mine purchased and was renovating in 2010. I was mesmerized by the hand-written words spilled across the yellowed pages of the diary, dusty with age, and only initials used for the entries, "D.T." My guess is the *fictional* character in my book, named *Gloria,* was the owner of the diary.

I researched a few things, and came to the conclusion that there was indeed a scandal in 1956 in this close-knit community. I took the events described and created a work of fiction. There are some triggers in this book, and some graphic scenes which are not meant to be superfluous, but to reinforce the magnitude of duplicity, abuse of power combined with the almost charismatic quality this evil person possessed. It was a different time, but then again, this type of conduct exists today. I merely wrote this piece of fiction, updating it to a more modern time, to affirm that evil comes in many forms. Nothing can ever change that, but perhaps eyes will be opened.

Excerpt from "Southern Comfort"

Avery Dawson switched on the porch light and peered out into the night. He turned his head to the side so that his eyes could catch a glimpse of the street, all the way to the corner. But there was nothing but darkness.

Mosquitoes and gnats were swirling around the porch light. He made a mental note to buy one of those bug zappers the next time he went to the hardware store.

The August night was quiet, thick with the Alabama humidity. The window air conditioner hummed noisily inside the living room, working hard to cool off the downstairs of their bungalow. There was another window unit upstairs in their bedroom. Sunny had one in her bedroom that was just across the hall from their room. She wasn't allowed to turn her A/C unit on until she was in the room for the night though and tonight she was late.

Again.

"Your sixteen-year-old has missed her curfew again, Donna. The girl has no respect for rules or boundaries it seems."

"Oh Avery," Donna replied, uncurling her tanned legs from beneath her as she sat upright on the sofa where she'd been glued to the television. "It's only eleven thirty-five. What's five or ten minutes?"

Avery turned to face her, his face a mask of solemnity. He was a man of God; he took rules and regulations seriously. He had done that all of his life. Having grown up in Tupelo, Mississippi, under the strict tutelage of his father, also a minister in the Southern Baptist faith, he had learned those lessons. He had been taught the importance of adhering to the rules, and conversely the consequences of defiance.

Sometimes those consequences culminated in having a razor strap flayed against his bare back. But at the end, he had learned the lessons he was supposed to learn; and he was raised with discipline. As a result, he respected the authority of those in power; God, of course, being the highest one. It was because of this he'd made a vow to serve God and see to it that others learned to follow the straight and narrow path that would ultimately lead them to their own personal salvation.

"The point, Donna, is that the girl needs to learn to follow the rules she's been given. Not to bend them at her whim. Five or ten minutes now, fifteen or twenty minutes next time. She has to learn self-discipline. You aren't consistent with discipline. She knows what she can get away with when it comes to you." His voice carried disapproval.

"But it's summer time. It's when she's supposed to cut loose a little bit, honey. Wouldn't hurt if we extended her curfew to midnight. My boy was allowed to stay out later on the weekends than she is at the same age, darlin'."

Avery had now tensed up. Donna was too soft where her offspring were concerned. That had been evident from their first date two years ago. The boy was obviously out of control. It had been a blessing when he finally enlisted in the military a year after graduating high school. Perhaps the Navy would find a way to repair the damage done as a result of his undisciplined upbringing.

But it wasn't too late for Sunny. Avery needed to press that upon Donna; he wanted to be a part of that process. He felt responsible now that he was part of this family to ensure that the girl reached her full spiritual potential. It was too easy these days to fall in with the wrong crowd and she had. They were wild party girls. In particular, Gina Margolis. He knew plenty about that one.

"Do you trust me?" he asked, as his grey eyes searched hers. "Because this is serious and I won't have you making light of it."

"Well, of course I do, Avery. I mean, I know that I haven't been a perfect parent with my kids, but gosh almighty, I mostly had to do it on my own."

"I understand that, sugar. But I'm here now and I'd like to think that I represent a good male influence in Sunny's life. One that she's been missing all of these years. It's not too late to instill some values in her and discipline will enforce that. She needs to learn by accepting the consequences of poor choices and bad decisions."

"Discipline?" Donna's forehead wrinkled with confusion. "Well it isn't as if I don't punish her for breaking the rules, Avery. I try to pick my battles, you know? I don't want to go to war with my only daughter. I remember how that had been with my own mama." She shuddered at the memories that surfaced. Her mother had never approved of one damn thing she had done her entire life. She hadn't wanted that to be the way it was between her and her own daughter.

Avery pulled Donna up from the sofa to stand before him. He framed her face with his large hands. "Listen, Donna. This is important now. You and me? Well, we need to do this together. We're a family or at least that's what I thought you wanted us to be."

"Oh, I do Avery! You know that I do."

"Okay then, you will need to trust my judgment on this. With the crowd of trash she's running with, well, we have no idea what she's been doing. Drinking? Smoking dope? Let's start with curfew, okay? She has to learn there are disciplinary consequences when she breaks the rules. Do you understand?"

Donna nodded. "Yes, Avery. I understand. You do what you think is best. I trust your judgment on this. I don't want to fail my children. I meant to be a good mother, I truly did."

"I know, sugar. And believe me, I'm not sitting in judgment of you, not for a second. But you didn't have a man around most of the time, and that's where it was difficult for you to be both mother and father to your children. Just remember that discipline is a form of love. And it is for her own good, Donna. You need to remember that."

She nodded. She knew that Avery was a good man with high moral standards. She was lucky to have him in her life; to ground her and influence her own behavior. Her past was one she wasn't proud of but Avery hadn't judged her at all. He had taken to her despite the sullied reputation she had earned along the way.

Her past wasn't pretty, there was no denying that. The men that had come and gone; the failed marriages that had led to her raising her children alone. She never wanted Avery to leave her. He was the best thing that could possibly have happened to her.

She even wanted to give him a child of his own. They hadn't discussed it, but she wasn't too old to fill that dream for him if he wanted. And if he did, well she was determined she would. Right now Avery was focused on getting his congregation established, but Donna knew that a child on the way would be a welcome distraction for both of them. She was sure of it.

Avery walked over to the front window and peered out again. She could tell there was still no sign of Sunny. "I think grounding her is in order when she decides to grace us with her presence tonight. You go on to bed now. I'll wait up for her."

"Are you sure?" Donna asked tentatively, chewing on her bottom lip in apprehension.

"I am. Go on up to bed. I'll wake you once she's home." She turned and started up the staircase, turning back to face him once more. "Goodnight then, Avery."

How about a brand new release by M.J. Rigel and me?

Synopsis

Charlie "Chip" Rose is just sixteen, the oldest of four children in a dysfunctional family. He has reason to have a chip on his shoulder (no pun intended) when he finds himself repeatedly the recipient of the consequences caused by his parents' poor decisions.

Chip strives for some normalcy in his life, but that is not on the horizon when his father goes to prison for what he's been growing out on the edge of their rural property. Chip has to take on the role of *man of the house*, as his mother struggles to make ends meet for the family.

But Chip still has his dreams; and though it is difficult for him to hide his resentment toward his family at times, he bides his time until he can put his plan into action. That happens the summer going into his senior year of high school. Finally, he may be able to use his training to bring in the finances he will need to go out on his own after graduation.

Finally, he can *live it up!*

About the Author

ANDREA SMITH IS A *USA Today* Best-Selling Author of more than thirty fiction novels. She has a wicked sense of humor, and no matter the genre, she is able to infuse laughter throughout.

She self-publishes Contemporary Romance, Romantic Suspense, Romantic Comedy, New Adult Romance, New Adult Suspense, Rock Star Romance, MMF Romance, MM Romance, True Crime Fiction and Sensual Romance with a paranormal twist. Her biggest fear is being a one-trick pony with her fiction. Endless numbers of books in one series would drive her crazy! She has so much more to imagine! Many of her books are also available on audio!

Don't miss out!

Visit the website below and you can sign up to receive emails whenever Andrea Smith publishes a new book. There's no charge and no obligation.

https://books2read.com/r/B-A-DYO-UAXGB

BOOKS 2 READ

Connecting independent readers to independent writers.

Did you love *Dirty Diana*? Then you should read *Crossing Lines*[1] by Andrea Smith!

[2]

When is love wrong?Jesse Ryan has always been the love of my life, from as far back as I can remember. But time, distance and circumstances beyond my control separated the two of us for many years.Now things have changed. Because you see now I'm a grown woman, and it's time that Jesse sees that for himself. But will he see me as anything other than the child I was when we last saw one another? It's up to me to make sure that he does.Look out Jesse Ryan. September is back!ADULT CONTENT

---

1. https://books2read.com/u/mgEYLz

2. https://books2read.com/u/mgEYLz

Read more at www.andreasmithauthor.com.

Also by Andrea Smith

ALPHAS IN LOVE
Taz

Beyond Series
Silent Whisper
Broken Dreams

Dream Series
Shadows & Dreams
These Dreams
Shattered Dreams
Dream Lover

Evermore Series
Crushed
Claimed

Paparazzi
Star F*cking

Forbidden Series
Loving Jesse
Crossing Lines
Forever Jesse
The Love Effect

G-Man
Carson: The Untold Story

G-Man Next Generation
Walk of Shame

G-Men: Next Generation
Dude Interrupted

Limbo
Stolen Dreams

M/M ALPHAS
Blacklisted
Quid Pro Quo

MMF Sandwich
Triple Play
Double Header
My Men Duet

Naughty Nuggets
Santa's Stocking Stuffers

Standalone
The Preacher
Dream Series Box Set
Murders On The Ridge
Bitch Games: We All Play Them
The Other Man
Wasted
All of Me
Love in Limbo Anthology
Dirty Diana
She's a Doll
Evermore

The Bug Guy

Watch for more at www.andreasmithauthor.com.

www.ingramcontent.com/pod-product-compliance
Lightning Source LLC
Chambersburg PA
CBHW051447130726
47987CB00005B/2222